THE Notorious DR. MACT

Other Books by Anna Durand

The British Bastard (A Hot Scots Prequel)
Dangerous in a Kilt (Hot Scots, Book One)
Wicked in a Kilt (Hot Scots, Book Two)
Scandalous in a Kilt (Hot Scots, Book Three)
The MacTaggart Brothers Trilogy (Hot Scots, Books 1-3)
Gift-Wrapped in a Kilt (Hot Scots, Book Four)
Notorious in a Kilt (Hot Scots, Book Five)
Insatiable in a Kilt (Hot Scots, Book Six)
Lethal in a Kilt (Hot Scots, Book Seven)
Irresistible in a Kilt (Hot Scots, Book Eight)
Devastating in a Kilt (Hot Scots, Book Nine)
Spellbound in a Kilt (Hot Scots, Book Ten)
Incendiary in a Kilt (Hot Scots, Book Twelve)
Lachlan in a Kilt (The Ballachulish Trilogy, Book One)
Aidan in a Kilt (The Ballachulish Trilogy, Book Two)
Rory in a Kilt (The Ballachulish Trilogy, Book Three)
Brit vs. Scot (A Hot Brits/Hot Scots/Au Naturel Crossover Book)
The American Wives Club (A Hot Brits/Hot Scots/Au Naturel Crossover Book)
One Hot Chance (Hot Brits, Book One)
One Hot Roomie (Hot Brits, Book Two)
One Hot Crush (Hot Brits, Book Three)
The Dixon Brothers Trilogy (Hot Brits, Books 1-3)
One Hot Escape (Hot Brits, Book Four)
One Hot Rumor (Hot Brits, Book Five)
One Hot Christmas (Hot Brits, Book Six)
One Hot Scandal (Hot Brits, Book Seven)
One Hot Deal (Hot Brits, Book Eight)
Natural Obsession (Au Naturel Nights, Book One)
Natural Passion (Au Naturel Trilogy, Book One)
Natural Impulse (Au Naturel Trilogy, Book Two)
Natural Satisfaction (Au Naturel Trilogy, Book Three)
Fired Up (standalone romance)
Echo Power (Echo Power Trilogy, Book One)
Echo Dominion (Echo Power Trilogy, Book Two)
Echo Unbound (Echo Power Trilogy, Book Three)
The Mortal Falls (Undercover Elementals, Book One)
The Mortal Fires (Undercover Elementals, Book Two)
The Mortal Tempest (Undercover Elementals, Book Three)
The Janusite Trilogy (Undercover Elementals, Books 1-3)
Obsidian Hunger (Undercover Elementals, Book Four)
Unbidden Hunger (Undercover Elementals, Book Five)
The Thirteenth Fae (Undercover Elementals, Book Six)
Echo Power (Echo Power Trilogy, Book One)
Echo Dominion (Echo Power Trilogy, Book Two)
Echo Unbound (Echo Power Trilogy, Book Three)
Passion Never Dies: The Complete Reborn Series

THE Notorious DR. MACT

A Hot Scots Prequel

ANNA DURAND

JACOBSVILLE BOOKS — MARIETTA, OHIO

THE NOTORIOUS DR. MacT

ISBN: 978-1-949406-97-9 (paperback)
ISBN: 978-1-949406-98-6 (ebook)
ISBN: 978-1-949406-99-3 (audiobook)

Manufactured in the United States.

Jacobsville Books
www.JacobsvilleBooks.com

Publisher's Cataloging-in-Publication Data
provided by Five Rainbows Cataloging Services

Names: Durand, Anna, author.
Title: The notorious Dr. MacT / Anna Durand.
Description: Marietta, OH : Jacobsville Books, 2021. | Series: Hot Scots prequel, bk. 1.
Identifiers: ISBN 978-1-949406-97-9 (paperback) | ISBN 978-1-949406-98-6
     (ebook) | ISBN 978-1-949406-99-3 (audiobook)
Subjects: LCSH: College teachers--Fiction. | Man-woman relationships--Fiction.
     | Scots--Fiction. | Americans--Fiction. | Romance fiction. | BISAC: FICTION
     / Romance / Contemporary. | FICTION / Romance / Romantic Comedy. |
     GSAFD: Love stories.
Classification: LCC PS3604.U724 N68 2021 (print) | LCC PS3604.U724 (ebook) |
     DDC 813/.6--dc23.

Chapter One

Iain

I march across the campus of Nackington University, head held high, shoulders back, and ignore the taunts and jeers erupting around me. I expect this reaction whenever I dress like a true Scotsman in a heathen country. I'd never been to America until I flew in last week, in preparation for assuming my new job as a professor of archaeology and ancient history.

"Whoa, dude," one young numpty shouts. He points at my clothing. "Do you wear lace panties too? They'd go with your plaid skirt."

It's a kilt, not a skirt. But I won't waste my time explaining that to any of these morons. Not everyone disapproves of my attire, though. The lasses love it. I see groups of them gathering to watch me stroll by and to whisper to each other while they give me appreciative glances.

Another laddie points at me and laughs. "What a dweeb. Did you lose a bet and had to wear a skirt to class today?"

I reach down to pat the hilt of my *sgian dubh* which pokes out of my sock. "My knife is bigger than yours, laddie."

Aye, I say the word knife as if I mean "dick." The laddie understands, I think, since he rolls his eyes. I prefer the word *slat*, since that's the Gaelic term.

My march through the asinine world of college laddies ends when I push through the double doors into the humanities building. The students milling about in the hall glance at me sideways but make no comment on my outfit. The lasses, naturally, cast me appreciative glances.

I find my classroom and walk up to the lectern that's been set up at the front of the room. The space is not large, but then, archaeology courses aren't normally the most popular ones. Still, I should have about thirty students this semester for my course on Celtic history. Aye, an American university offers a class like that. They created it this year just for me because I convinced the curriculum committee that the university should expand its offerings. They were keen on the idea. Very keen.

Turns out the grandparents of the committee chairman emigrated from Scotland.

And now I have emigrated too, though only for a while. I've been given a one-year contract with the option to extend it if everyone likes my work here.

I set my bag on the floor beside the lectern and get set up for today's class. Someone walks into the room just as I'm finishing. I see the figure peripherally, and since I'm still organizing my papers on the lectern, I speak without glancing up. "*Guten Morgen.*"

"Uh, good morning?"

The female voice bears a note of uncertainty.

I lift my head and see a bonnie lass standing halfway across the room. She's more than bonnie. The auburn beauty transfixes me with her voluptuous figure and her classical features. Since I've confused her, I say, "*Guten Morgen* is German for good morning."

"Oh. *Guten Morgen*, then." She moves closer, halting an arm's length away. "You don't sound German, though."

"I'm Scottish." I step sideways, away from the lectern, and offer her my hand. "Iain MacTaggart."

She slips her hand into mine. "Rae Everhart."

"A pleasure to meet you, Rae." I step behind the lectern again. "I learned some German phrases while doing field work in the Saxony region."

"Wow. That must be amazing. To work in another country, I mean. I've never been anywhere except America."

"You'll get to know Scotland in this class." I wink. "It's a very romantic country."

Am I flirting with her? She's a student, an undergraduate, which means she cannae be more than twenty-one or twenty-two. A thirty-seven-year-old man should not be making romantic advances toward a lass fifteen years his junior.

More students begin to file into the room.

"Choose a seat," I tell Rae. "Class will start shortly."

She sits down three rows back, directly in front of me. I don't watch the other students as they choose their seats. No, I can't stop staring at Rae. Her eyes are the most entrancing shade of dark blue I've ever seen. Her lips have just enough fullness to make them enticing too, and I know I could kiss those lips for hours. But I won't do that. Getting sacked for sexual misconduct on my first day at Nackington would ruin my career.

I can be mates with a student, though. Can't I?

Once everyone has taken a seat, I set my hands on the edges of the lectern and begin. "Good morning. I'm Dr. Iain MacTaggart, your teacher for the semester. Welcome to Celtic History 401, the Story of Scotland from the Paleolithic Era to the Union of Crowns." I raise a hand just as a lad raises his hand to ask a question. "Donnae worry. In due course, I will explain the meanings of those terms and many more. By the end of this semester, you'll be experts on all these subjects."

"Cool," a blonde lass declares. "I love your accent, by the way."

"Thank you." My gaze gravitates to Rae. The second our eyes meet, she smiles. "Let's dive into the first lesson."

Her lips tighten more, carving out dimples in her cheeks.

Bod an Donais, the lass is lovely. Kissing her would be…cause for my dismissal. Aye, I *should* curse myself in Gaelic because only an erse would think about kissing a student.

I clear my throat and focus on the class. The girls all watch me with rapt attention while the boys thumb through their textbooks or scribble in their notebooks, though I suspect they're not taking notes. Aye, getting and keeping the attention of college students is always a challenge. Before I can begin my lecture, I ask for the names of all the students and write them down on the diagram of the classroom that I made last night. I also inform them they should always sit in the same seat because that will make it easier for me to remember their names. And aye, one sarcastic young man asks if I have senile dementia and that's why I need a chart to remember the students' names. I shake my head and do not respond.

Stepping out from behind the lectern, I gesture at my clothing. "I'm sure you're all wondering about the way I'm dressed."

"Yeah, what's up with the skirt?" a cheeky sod asks.

I feign disappointment. "Apparently, none of the lads in America know any other way to insult a Scot. You all say the same thing. I expected better from seniors who will graduate in the spring and go on to exciting careers in the fast food industry."

The laddie clamps his jaw shut and puckers his lips, staring down at his notebook.

I take hold of my kilt and lift it just enough to reveal my knees, though I didn't do it for that purpose. I meant to draw their attention to the garment. "This is a kilt. Not a skirt. The kilt I'm wearing features the MacTaggart clan tartan. Every clan distinguishes itself with a unique plaid design." I pull my knife out of my sock and raise it for the class to see. "This is a *sgian dubh*, a type of dagger used as a weapon by Scots in the old days. Today, it's strictly for ornamental use. The word *sgian dubh* means 'black knife.' No one knows why, but that's what we call these blades."

Rae raises her hand.

I nod to her. "What's your question?"

"Do you have a big sword too?"

When a few laddies make suggestive noises, Rae bows her head.

I glare at each snickering *cacan* in turn—and they all haud their wheesht. Wee shits always crumble under pressure. Now that I've silenced them, I focus on Rae. "Aye, I do have a sword back home in Scotland. My cousin Lachlan gave it to me for my birthday last year." I squint at the laddies who had ridiculed Rae and speak in a menacingly soft voice. "My sword is called a claymore, and with that blade, I could take the head off anyone who causes trouble."

I wave my *sgian dubh* in a threatening gesture.

The laddies pick up their pens and pencils as if they now mean to pay attention to the lesson without harassing anyone. Maybe I enjoyed terrifying them a bit too much, but I cannae stand for any man harassing a woman.

Rae tentatively raises her hand again.

"Go on," I say. "What did you want to ask?"

"Um…" She bites her upper lip. "I was wondering about your shirt. It's cool, but it doesn't look old-timey."

"No, it's not. I didn't have a traditional shirt, so I improvised." I wink at her. "If I can find a Jacobite kilt shirt, I'll wear it to class one day."

She smiles shyly, and it's the sweetest thing I've ever seen.

"All right," I say, stepping behind the lectern again. "It's time to dig into our first lesson for this week—the Paleolithic Era. Does anyone know what that term means?"

A laddie, identified on my chart as Andy, thrusts his hand up.

"Tell me your definition, Andy."

"It's a pail of lithic. You know, like a bucket full of, uh…lithic stuff."

"Afraid not. Anyone else care to try?"

No one moves. Most of them stare at me blankly.

Then Rae lifts her hand. When I nod, she says, "Paleolithic means 'old stone.' So the Paleolithic Era is the Old Stone Age, meaning that the people then used only stone tools. The Mesolithic and Neolithic came after that but before the invention of metalworking."

"Excellent, Rae. That's a perfect definition."

She sits up straighter, and her lips curl into a lovely little smile.

While I continue my lecture, the other students get more involved as they become more comfortable with me. I might be Scottish, and I might be wearing a kilt and a *sgian dubh*, but I am not a frightening man. I discuss the Paleolithic in Scotland, and my students actually take notes and ask questions. This is a good start. I had worried that the students might not accept me readily, but those fears have evaporated.

Especially when I look at Rae.

Christ, I should not be thinking about her this much. She's a student and far too young for me.

Rae stays behind after the other students have left the room. She approaches me as I'm putting all my notes and pictures into my attaché case. «Dr. MacTaggart?»

"Please call me Iain."

She hunches her shoulders and smiles shyly again, which makes me want to kiss her right now. "Okay, Iain."

"Did ye have a question, lass?"

Rae nods. "I wondered if today was the only time you'll talk about the Paleolithic. I'm really interested in that era."

"Aye, this was the only in-class lecture on that topic. But I'd be happy to discuss it with you outside of class."

"You mean like a tutoring type thing?"

No, because I hadn't thought that far ahead. The words poured out of me before I'd bothered to consider them. What's the harm in tutoring a student outside of class? Rae wants to know more about the Paleolithic, that's all. I won't get so randy that I'll seduce her. I might find her attractive, but I have self-control.

"Aye," I say. "A tutoring thing."

She grins. "That would be fantastic. Thank you, Iain."

"My pleasure, Rae. We could start at four o'clock today, if you're free."

"Yeah, I'm free."

"Let's meet at the campus museum. I can tutor you while we look at actual relics from that era."

Her grins gets even bigger. "I love museums."

A student who loves museums? I've never met anyone like her before. None of my pupils back in Scotland would've begged for extra work outside of class. But Rae honestly wants to learn more about my country's ancient past—and I honestly want to teach her about that.

We walk out of the classroom together, then go our separate ways. At four o'clock this afternoon, I will meet Rae for what might turn out to be the first of many tutoring sessions. She seems very keen on learning as much as possible. I don't even know what type of degree she's working to achieve, but I can tell she will excel at anything she tries.

For the rest of the day, until four p.m. arrives, I keep glancing at every clock I see. And I keep thinking about Rae Everhart.

Chapter Two

Rae

Iain MacTaggart is the hottest man on earth. Okay, maybe that's hyperbole, but I don't care. I love his pale blue eyes, his light brown hair, and that hook nose. He has the kind of rugged sex appeal that I never knew I'd love—but I do. I'd never met anyone like Iain until today. He's a real man, the kind every woman secretly dreams about but thinks she'll never find.

Oh God. I've turned into one of those girls I used to make fun of, the ones who drool over every guy they see.

Though I love my classes, my mind keeps wandering back to Dr. Iain MacTaggart. He's an amazing teacher, and I'm not just saying that because I have a crush on him. He makes ancient history exciting and entertaining, especially when he smiles with devilish humor right before he makes a joke. Yeah, Iain is electrifying.

My last class of the day ends at four o'clock, so I rush over to the museum and burst through the main doors before I realize I shouldn't be sprinting into the lobby. I probably shouldn't have sprinted all the way from the math building, either. Now I'm breathing hard and my cheeks feel warm, a sure sign of overexertion. So I guzzle water from the fountain in the lobby, splashing a little on my face to cool me down. Jeez, Iain will think I'm insane or asthmatic or something.

Once I feel capable of speech again, I shuffle backward, away from the fountain.

And bump into someone.

I whirl around—and my heart thuds. "Oh, Iain. God, I'm so sorry I crashed into you."

"No worries." He smiles and winks. "My kilt protected me."

I glance at his kilt with a touch of skepticism. "Plaid has some kind of magic powers to save you from falling down and cracking your skull?"

"Aye. I've cast a *sain* on my kilt, and my *sgian dubh* is also my *luirgean*."

I stare at him, blinking slowly. "Are you speaking another language?"

"Scots Gaelic. I said I've cast a charm on my kilt, and my knife is also my magic staff."

For some stupid reason, I glance down at his groin.

Iain hooks a finger under my chin and lifts until our gazes meet. "My magic staff is my knife, remember?"

He spoke those words in a sensual tone. Or maybe I imagined it was sexy because I'm so insanely attracted to him. Did he realize I was staring at his other 'magic staff'? Not that I can see it. Well, I did notice a slight bulge down there.

Snap out of it, girl.

Iain turns to the side and waves for me to go with him. "Let's start our tour of the Nackington Museum of History with the Paleolithic exhibits."

He leads the way until we enter the Hall of Prehistory, then he slows down just enough that we can walk side by side. People give us funny looks, but I think they're baffled by his clothing, not horrified that an undergraduate is hanging out with a professor. He doesn't look thirty-seven. But I have no idea what someone of that age is supposed to look like. Maybe everybody in their late thirties has the same youthfulness and virility as Iain.

I assumed tutoring would involve Iain talking and me listening. But no, we have conversations. He shares what he knows about each exhibit, then invites me to ask questions which in turn becomes a back and forth that's way more fun than sitting in class listening to a lecture. I love his voice. The man could recite the instructions for performing an appendectomy, and I'd still swoon.

Not that I have swooned. Maybe a little on the inside.

Once our tour has ended, Iain suggests we go to the museum's café to «have a piece.» Turns out that means to have a snack, preferably a sandwich. But when we get to the café, I want something sweet, and Iain goes along with that. We sit on either side of a round table and talk some more while we enjoy our cinnamon rolls. He tells me about Scotland and makes me laugh so hard that I accidentally spit out a glob of half-chewed pastry. It gets stuck on my chin.

Iain reaches over the table to wipe my chin off with a napkin.

None of the other guys I've known would do that. Iain is a gentleman on top of being hot and funny and surprisingly sweet. I've only slept with two boys in my life so far, and neither of them could hold a candle to the hot Scot. I'd love for him to kiss me, but he hasn't even tried to do that. Well, we are in a public place. I shouldn't want him to kiss me, but I can't help it. My body craves things I'd never even thought about until today. Naughty, dirty things.

Oh yeah, tonight I'll need to break out my vibrator and get off while fantasizing about Iain MacTaggart.

He insists on driving me to my apartment off-campus, since my old car died and I haven't bought a newer used vehicle yet, which means I've been taking the bus. But he says goodbye on the sidewalk just outside my building without touching me in any way, not even to shake my hand. I make my way up to the second floor of the complex and into the apartment I share with my roommate, Cecilia Bremner-Ashton aka Cece. I've only known her for a week, and I can't tell yet what kind of roomie she'll be. The girl seems kind of uptight and snobby. She's from a rich family, and her father is the university's largest donor. I learned that from Cece herself. She loves to brag about her family's wealth and status. I've heard rumors that the Bremner-Ashtons are powerful and almost like a Midwest mafia, but I've always dismissed that as gossip.

I do know, because Cece told me, that her parents insisted she should live on her own while attending Nackington University, rather than in their mansion. Maybe she annoys her family too.

I've just dropped my backpack on the living room table when Cece ambles out of her bedroom wearing her favorite silk teddy.

She yawns and stretches. "Where have you been? Thought your last class ended at four."

"I went to the campus museum."

Cece's lip curls. "Why would anybody do that? It's so…nerdy."

"That's me. I'm a nerd." I kick my shoes off and flop onto the sofa, resting my feet on the coffee table. "Did you eat yet? We could order pizza."

"Eat? It's only six thirty."

"Yeah, and I'm hungry. Aren't you?"

She rolls her eyes. "Nobody worth knowing eats dinner before eight o'clock."

I grew up in a completely different way than Cece did. My family ate breakfast at seven, lunch at noon, and dinner at six every day. I'm sure my snooty roommate thinks that schedule is hopelessly bourgeois. I mean, my family didn't even have a butler, much less a chef or a team of maids. Whether Cece's family is happy, I don't know. Mine isn't. Maybe my parents haven't been the happiest people, but I always believed they loved me and each other. Until this past summer. That's when I found out my parents had been separated for six months and had just filed for divorce. Mom didn't want to tell me what had happened, but I pushed until she confessed that Dad had been cheating on her for years. She finally couldn't take it anymore. I don't blame her. Dad hooked up with a slut two years older than I am, and now they're living together.

I know Mom loves me. But Dad… I don't want to think about him anymore, not today. I had a wonderful day at school and especially with Iain. So I'm going to focus on that and forget the bad stuff.

Grabbing the cordless phone off the end table, I start to dial a number. "I'm ordering pizza. Do you want some or not?"

Cece wrinkles her nose. "No thank you. I'm having dinner with a boy. At a restaurant. Five star."

Does Nackington, Wisconsin, have a five-star restaurant? I kind of doubt that. It's a small town, not a metropolis. If she wants to lie about where she's going and with whom, the girl can go for it. I don't care what she does. So I order a large ham pizza with extra cheese. Yeah, I'm going to eat the whole thing myself. I add a small dessert pizza to my order too. Pigging out sounds awesome right now. The time I spent with Iain today left me feeling invigorated and ravenous. Since I can't get it on with my professor, I'll stuff my face instead.

Cece and I lounge on the sofa to watch her favorite reality shows while I eat my meal. I can't stand these shows, but I'm trying to be a good roommate. If we're going to share an apartment for ten months, I need to learn the fine art of compromise.

My roomie doesn't seem to care about that.

During a commercial break, Cece turns toward me. Her smile seems kind of sneaky. "Soooo, I was looking out the window earlier, and I saw you and your new boy toy."

"Boy toy? I've never had one of those."

She leans toward me, seeming almost excited, and whispers, "The guy in plaid. Who is he?"

"One of my professors. He teaches Celtic history."

Her nose wrinkles. "Who wants to learn about that? Only dweebs like you."

"Uh-huh." Let her say what she wants. I don't care.

Cece seems even more excited now, like a dog that just found a juicy bone. "Are you screwing him? I mean, he's jalapeño hot. If you aren›t going to tap that, maybe I will.»

She is so not Iain's type. Right, like I know what kind of girls he prefers. But I just can't picture him screwing an uptight snob like Cece.

I roll my eyes to indicate the clock on the wall. "Shouldn't you get ready for your big five-star date?"

"Yep." She leaps off the sofa and trots toward the hallway. "Don't be jealous. I'm sure some pimply geek will snatch you up any day now."

Does she hate me? Or is she like this with everyone? I've never done anything to her, but I'm getting sick of her snide comments and nosiness.

Once my roomie leaves, I shut off the TV and go into my bedroom. I take care of my homework, then change into my nightie, intending to go to sleep. But I toss and turn, my mind racing with thoughts of Iain. When he had leaned in and said, in that rough and sexy voice, that his "magic staff" is his knife, I'd wanted to jump him right then. I swear I'm not that kind of girl. But Iain makes me feel so many things I've never experienced before. Maybe the reason I've only slept with two guys, and each time it was only once, is because I hadn't met a man like Iain MacTaggart.

I know I'll never get any sleep unless I can do something about the wet ache between my thighs. So I yank the nightstand drawer open and pull out my vibrator.

Shimmying under the sheets, I lift my nightie's hem up to my hips and spread my legs. Then I slide the vibrator between my folds and switch it on, using the lowest setting. I stroke it up and down my cleft while I grow slicker and my breaths quicken. I imagine Iain kneeling between my thighs, naked and aroused, whispering filthy things to me, and I can't stop myself from cranking the vibrator up a few notches.

Iain. Naked. Thrusting into me.

My back arches, and I thrust the vibrator into me, pushing it deep and hard while I fist my free hand in the sheets and start panting. But I need that finger, so I release the sheets and rub my clit furiously, fucking myself with the vibrator so hard that I hear a wet sucking sound every time I pull it out and plunge it back inside me. I can't breathe, can't stop, can't slow down, need to come so badly. The bed starts to creak, my body curls in on itself, and I'm teetering on the edge of an invisible cliff, about to tumble off it and free-fall into bliss. The climax hits me so hard that the breath I'd been holding explodes out of me, and strangled cries spill from my lips while wave after wave pulsates inside me. I pull out the vibrator and push my fingers inside to feel the contractions, which makes me come harder.

I lie here limp and tangled up in the sheets for I don't know how long. My chest heaves. My ears ring. Sweat drizzles down my temples. The vibrator still lies nestled between my thighs. Once I've caught my breath, I flip the sheets off me. Grabbing the vibrator, I go into the bathroom to wash it off and pee. I hadn't really needed to go until I started masturbating, then the urge to pee grew stronger in time with my escalating need to come. Once I've relieved myself, I crawl back into bed.

And fall asleep in seconds.

Yeah, Iain MacTaggart gives me fantastic orgasms—and he's not even in the room with me.

Chapter Three

Iain

Last night, I dreamed of Rae. I wish I could claim those dreams were sweet and involved nothing more erotic than hand-holding. But no, the fantasies that assailed me while I slept involved Rae naked and writhing beneath me. Bloody hell, I won't get a good night's sleep until the semester is over and I won't need to see the lass anymore. When we met yesterday morning, Rae had seemed almost shy and definitely uncomfortable with talking to me. By late afternoon, when I saw her again, she had recovered her self-confidence. I enjoyed giving her a tour of the museum's Paleolithic exhibits more than I should have.

Why had I suggested we do that? I need to avoid Rae, not spend more time with her.

Just as I'm finishing my breakfast, alone in my flat, my mobile phone rings. I answer without checking who might be calling.

"Iain, *gràidh*, how are ye settling in?" my mother asks. "America is so far from home."

"Aye, I know that. Donnae worry, Ma, I'm doing fine here." Meeting Rae has been a joy and a catastrophe. No, not a catastrophe. But being with her does test my willpower. "How are things at home? Is Da keeping out of trouble?"

"Oh, aye. Angus is well."

"What about you?"

"Nothing to complain about. Are ye sure nothing's fashing ye?"

I can't tell my mother the truth. She wouldn't understand why I'm "tutoring" a college senior, a beautiful one who makes me want to do things that would get me sacked. So I stick with banal subjects. "Nothing is fashing me, Ma. I taught my first classes yesterday, and everything went well. The students needed a wee bit of time to get used to me, but then they were highly engaged."

"Ye mean they liked ye."

"Aye, that's what I mean." I glance at the clock on the microwave oven. "I need to go. More classes to teach today."

We say goodbye, and I dress for my second day at Nackington. This time, I wear normal clothes that won't make my students ask why I'm wearing a plaid skirt. I don't care what they think, but I never intended to wear the kilt all the time. I walk out of my flat dressed in trousers and a button-down shirt, though I leave the top button undone to avoid seeming stuffy. As I stride across the campus to reach the humanities building, lasses whistle at me. Cannae help smirking at that. I was never this popular with women back in Loch Fairbairn, my hometown in Scotland. Aye, the lasses liked me. But they did not whistle and wink at me while smiling suggestively.

I don't remember university being like this when I'd been a student.

As I push through the doors into the humanities building, I bump into Rae. Literally.

She smiles and bites her lip. "Sorry, Iain. I didn't see you coming."

"The doors are tinted to reduce glare. So it's easy not to notice what's on the other side."

"You know the doors are tinted?" Her smile broadens. "You must be the only professor on campus who knows things like that."

"I'd wager the janitorial staff know. They clean the doors and windows, after all." Why the bloody hell am I havering about tinted glass? I've turned into an eejit, all because I bumped into Rae. "Well, I should get to class."

"Me too."

We brush past each other, then both glance back at the same time.

And I become worse than an eejit. I mutate into a dafty and ask, "Would you like to have another tutoring session at the museum? We could visit the Egyptian exhibits this time."

Her expression lights up. "Oh, I love ancient Egypt. Yeah, let's do that."

"Four o'clock again?"

"Sure." She grins. "Can't wait to see y—Um, see that exhibit."

Had she been about to say she can't wait to see me again? I'm a mature man, not a randy laddie, but I suddenly feel like a teenager again. Rae does this to me. And I can't wait to see that "exhibit" again too.

This morning, my first class is about archaeology in the UK. I love this topic, and I do my best to make it interesting and entertaining for my students, but thoughts of Rae keep slipping into my mind unbidden. Maybe I enjoy those thoughts a wee bit too much, but I've decided not to chastise myself for that. Thoughts can't be controlled. I learned that from a lass I dated during my doctoral program. She was training to be a school counselor, so she studied a lot about psychology.

Now that I've given myself permission to think of Rae, I feel more relaxed. The rest of the day seems to go by swiftly, and I'm glad for that. Not because I know I'll see Rae in forty-five minutes. Teaching can be tiring, and a museum visit will be relaxing.

I arrive at the museum to find Rae is already there, waiting in the lobby. She smiles when she sees me pushing through the doors. I smile and wave to her. She trots up to me, and I lay a hand on the small of her back as we meander through the museum to find the Egyptian gallery. Laying a hand on her was a reflex. I shouldn't have done that, I suppose, but it's a show of respect for women in general, not a suggestion that I want to shag her. Still, I pull my hand away as we enter the Hall of Egyptian History.

We amble through the exhibits, but I have trouble finding anything to say that she doesn't already know. Rae clearly has a deep interest in ancient Egypt. Since I can't impress her with my knowledge of the subject, I take a different tack.

"Do you know what the name Hatshepsut means?" I ask.

Rae angles her head to look at me. "No. Do you? I know she ascended the throne to become pharaoh in the Eighteenth Dynasty."

"Aye. But Hatshepsut means 'foremost of noble women.' She portrayed herself as a man in depictions on temple walls."

"It's cool that you know stuff like that."

"Name meanings are of great interest to me." I suddenly realize I've laid a hand on her back again and pull it away. "Sorry. I should've asked permission before doing that."

"Doing what?"

"Touching you."

She stares at me for a few seconds, her eyes wide and her expression blank. Then she laughs gently. "You mean when you put your hand on my back. I'm not annoyed about that. I think it's kind of sweet that you do that."

"Kind of sweet? You can tell me I'm a bloody erse for doing that. I won't be upset."

"What is an 'erse'?"

I exhale a long sigh. "An ass."

Rae shakes her head slowly while her lips curve into a soft smile. She places a hand on my cheek. "You are not an ass, Iain. I love that you're an old-fashioned gentleman. Most guys these days don't hold doors open for women, and they don't even bother to wait for a girl to catch up to them. They just hustle off."

"Are all American men such erseholes?"

"No. Just most of them." She pats my cheek. "But not you."

"Well, at least I've done better than most men in this country. It takes an old man like me to treat a woman like a lady."

"Old man?" She folds her arms over her chest and scans me up and down. "You don't look ancient. Mind if I ask how old you are? Since you mentioned age."

"Donnae mind at all. I'm thirty-seven."

"Really?" She feigns shock. "You *are* an old fogy. Should I get one of those electric buggies for you? The kind they have in grocery stores. Don't want you to have a stroke."

"Very funny, ye cheeky lass." I pretend to study her intently, tapping a finger on my chin. "How old are you? Maybe you're nothing but a bairn."

"A what?" she says with a laugh.

"It means a child. Scots call them bairns."

"You're in America now. Try using our words." She bumps her shoulder into me. "You might like it."

"Ah, perhaps." I glance at her sideways. "Since I'm a gentleman, I won't point out that you never told me your age."

"I'm not sensitive about that. I'm twenty-one, but I'll turn twenty-two in November."

Despite the fact I'd guessed as much, I still feel a chill rush over my skin when I hear her confirm it. I am flirting with a virtual bairn. Our fifteen-year age difference means I have become a dirty old man, the sort who seduces innocent young lasses and uses them for his own pleasure. Not that I've done anything of the sort with

Rae. Not yet. I want her, but I refuse to become just another pathetic sod who chases after young lasses.

Rae lifts her brows at me. "You seem shocked."

"No, I—It's not your age that fashes me. It's mine."

"Your age bothers you, but mine doesn't. That makes no sense."

"Aye." I wince and scratch my cheek. "But that's how I feel."

"So, you don't want to be my tutor anymore."

"I didn't say that." I should say it, but I can't make myself speak the words. Spending time with her feels like a breath of fresh air. After the troubles I'd endured back home, I need to breathe in every bit of warmth and sweetness she can give me. But… "We probably shouldn't see each other outside of class anymore."

"Why? It's not illegal to be friends with a student. Is it?"

"Not illegal, no. But I'm not sure about the university's code of ethics."

Her shoulders flag, and she looks down at the floor. "Okay. I understand."

But she sounds despondent. *Bod an Donais.* How am I meant to handle this situation? I suggested tutoring her, and now I've backed out and made the lass unhappy.

Rae lifts her gaze to mine, her eyes shining with the start of tears. "Guess I should go now. Sorry to have been so much trouble. It's just that I don't have any real friends and—Never mind."

The hitch in her voice makes my throat tighten.

She turns to walk away.

And I grasp her arm. "Donnae leave, Rae. I'm an erse for sure, and I overreacted to finding out how young you are. But I don't want to stop tutoring you."

She glances back at me with her glistening eyes. "Are you sure?"

"Yes, I'm sure. Let's enjoy the rest of the exhibits in this hall. If you still want to do that."

"Of course I do." She wipes at her eyes, and that lovely smile returns. "Let's go."

Maybe I've made a terrible mistake, but I don't care. How can I push away a sweet lass who only wants to spend time with me? I did suggest we do this. It's not her fault. No, I'm the dirty old man who lured an innocent young woman into my web. But I will behave like a professor and treat her like a student, no matter how much I want to kiss her and… No, I won't finish that thought.

Rae and I browse the rest of the Hall of Egyptian History, and she asks me what the names of pharaohs and officials mean. She thinks it's "adorable" that I'm fascinated by names and what they signify. Rae also announces that I am "so unbelievably sweet," though I don't understand why. She claims it's because I treat her with respect and haven't tried to "scam" my way into her "pants."

Do American college lads do things like that? They sound like bastards to me, and I can't imagine why any women want to sleep with them. I also can't believe she wants to tell me about those erses. I suppose it means she trusts me.

"Sometimes the bastards are the best at seducing a girl," Rae informs me when I voice my confusion over how American men behave. She hunches her shoulders and hugs herself. "I fell for it once. My sophomore year. I met this guy who seemed like he really wanted to get to know me better, and he was a pro at charming the pants off me. After we, you know, did the deed, he just vanished. A week later, I saw him making out with another girl. God, I was such an idiot."

"You are not stupid, Rae. Men like that deserve to be skelped. That means they should be smacked about."

She wraps her arms around herself more tightly. "Can't believe I told you all of that. You must be wishing you'd let me run away."

"No, I would never wish for that." We've stopped just outside the exit of the Egyptian exhibit hall. I brush a thumb over her chin. "Donnae waste any more time thinking about that wee shit. He's not worth your time."

"Thank you, Iain." She drops her arms and takes a deep breath, blowing it out. "I'm glad we're friends."

"So am I."

But for how long can I pretend I don't want more?

Chapter Four

Rae

Last night, I had a terrible dream that left me wondering if everything I've done recently had been a mistake. The things I'd done with Iain, that is. I dreamed that my father came for a visit and met Iain, and suddenly Iain realized I'm just a twenty-one-year-old student, and he told me I'm pathetic, then laughed at me. My dad made a joke about how young and stupid I am, believing that a grown man could want me. Iain laughed so hard at the joke that his eyes watered, and then both men pointed at me and laughed even harder.

Okay, it was a stress dream. I know that. But I can't shake the feeling that Iain really will realize I'm too young for a man like him to even hang out with me, much less…do things we can't do anyway. Because I'm a student. Because he's a professor.

All week long, I'd spent my late afternoons with Iain MacTaggart, perusing the campus museum and listening in rapt fascination while he explained the history and significance of every exhibit. Whenever I asked a question, he would smile and call me a "clever lass," then give me his answer. Twice he called me "sunshine," which made my cheeks feel as warm as the sun. I love that nickname. But why does he have to be so sexy? Why does his voice have to sound so rumbly and hot? I want to throw myself at him and crush my mouth to his.

But I can never do that. *Rats.*

At least I finally bought a car. No more bus rides that rattle my teeth. I hate that my mom paid for my new ride, but she insists I should not work while getting my degree. "Concentrate on your studies," she always tells me. I think she mostly feels bad that my father has zero interest in me.

Since it's the weekend now, I feel like doing something fun. By myself. I don't have any friends yet—unless I want to invite my roomie to go shopping with me. No, I don't think I'll do that. I doubt doing anything with Cece would qualify as a fun excursion. That means I'll explore the town of Nackington alone. Well, I've been alone here for three years. It's nothing new. Still, I miss my mom and the way we used to go on shopping trips together, though we rarely bought much. We just liked hanging out. But I won't see Mom again until Christmas break.

Cece is still asleep, so I leave a note telling her I'll be gone all day. I have no idea if she cares, but it seemed like the polite thing to do.

While I'm getting dressed for my day of solo shopping, my cell phone rings. I answer without glancing at the screen, engrossed in selecting the right pair of tennies. "Hello?"

"Guten Morgen, Rae."

My heart stutters. I swear it does. My pulse accelerates too, and for some reason, I lick my lips. "Good morning, Iain. How did you get my cell number?"

"You gave it to me yesterday. Remember?"

"Oh, yeah. I forgot."

He clears his throat, and his deep voice sounds a touch hesitant when he speaks again. "I was, ah, wondering if you have plans today."

"No, I don't." If he wants to take me somewhere, I will drop all my plans instantly, if I'd had any. Yeah, I'm pathetic. Especially since I want him to "take me" in the dirty sense of the phrase.

"Would you like to explore the town with me? I've only just moved here, but you must know the area."

"Actually, I don't. For the past three years, I've stuck to the places I needed to go—the campus, my apartment complex, the grocery store, stuff like that."

He says nothing for several seconds, then speaks in a deeper, sexier tone. "Then we can explore together."

Damn, Iain makes that statement sound so hot. But I doubt he meant it in a naughty way.

"Sure," I say. "Let's explore."

"I'll pick you up in an hour." He pauses. "But, ah, you'll need to give me your address. I forgot to write it down when I drove you home."

After I recite the address, we say goodbye—and I feel a ridiculous urge to change my clothes, the stuff I just put on five minutes ago. But I resist that impulse. I look fine. And if Iain doesn't like my outfit, that's tough.

Will he wear his kilt?

I roll my eyes at myself. Yeah, sure, because everybody dresses like a medieval Scot when they go sightseeing.

He picks me up in his car, and we spend several minutes just sitting in the parking lot while we discuss where we want to go. I had gotten online while I waited for him and looked up where the shops are in this town, as well as touristy sites. We finally agree on shopping first. Yeah, a man actually wants to do that. When I tease Iain about it, he smiles and calls me a "cheeky lass."

We visit several shops but don't buy anything, not until we walk into a novelty store that offers all kinds of silly gifts. Iain finds a T-shirt that he insists on buying for me. It features an ancient Egyptian design reminiscent of hieroglyphs with the words Nackington Museum of History printed on it.

"Thank you, Iain," I say while bouncing on my toes. "I love my new T-shirt."

His lips kink up at the corners. "I love how much you love that shirt."

I grin. "Maybe I should pick a T-shirt for you."

"Go on. I could use something new."

Wow. No other guy I've known would want a girl to pick out clothing for him. I hunt through the racks of T-shirts in search of one that seems appropriate for him. But I can't find anything that feels right. So I tell Iain to stay put while I scurry over to the checkout counter and ask the clerk if it's possible to get a custom-made shirt. He tells me, yeah, they can do it. I explain what I want, and the nice young man rushes into a back room to fulfill my order.

I can see Iain standing among the racks, watching me with a puzzled expression.

While I wait for my order, I trot back to Iain. We check out the racks of postcards, and he chooses a few to send home to his parents and some of his cousins.

"Are you an only child?" I ask.

"I am. But I have many cousins who are like brothers and sisters to me."

"Cool. I'm an only child too, but I don't have any cousins."

The store clerk has just emerged from the back room, and he waves for me to meet him at the checkout counter. Iain moves to follow me, but I slap a hand on his chest. "Wait here. It won't be a surprise if you see it before I'm ready to give it to you."

He smirks. "I've never seen you bossy before. It suits you."

I get a delicious glow in my chest when he says that, and when he smirks that way. I can feel the warmth and firmness of his chest too, thanks to my hand touching him. But I tear my hand away and jog over to the counter. The clerk has already put the gift into a bag, so I pay and take my surprise back to Iain.

He reaches for the bag.

I snatch it away. "Uh-uh-uh. Not until we're in the car."

The Scot makes a face that seems like a cross between annoyance and humor.

"Still like my bossiness?" I ask, bumping my shoulder into his.

"Aye, I still do."

We exit the shop and start down the sidewalk toward Iain's car, which is parked two blocks away on a cross street. As we pass another shop, Iain stops and moves to go inside, reaching for the door handle.

"Sure you want to do that?" I ask. Then I point to the sign above the door. "Did you read that?"

He glances up. His eyes go wide briefly, then he turns away and clears his throat. "Let's bypass this shop."

Yeah, I figured he hadn't noticed the sign. It says, "Adult Novelties."

We walk side-by-side back to his car, and he opens the passenger door for me like the gentleman he is. Once he's climbed into the driver's seat, he holds out his hand to me, palm up. "My gift now, please."

"Kinda anxious to find out what it is, huh?"

"Aye." He leans closer and speaks in a softer, deeper voice. "So give it to me now, Rae."

A thrill races over my skin whenever he uses that tone of voice. I hand him the bag.

He reaches inside to pull out his gift, unfolding the T-shirt so he can see the images and words printed on it. And he chuckles. "Real men wear plaid skirts? And there's a cartoon of a Scotsman dancing about in his kilt."

"Yeah. That seemed like the right gift for you."

"But you've never seen me dance."

"That was the best Scottish image the store clerk could find. I don't actually expect you to dance."

"Good. Because I have two left feet." He studies the shirt, and his lips curl up at the corners. "Thank you, Rae. It's a cheeky but thoughtful surprise."

"You're welcome."

He whips his shirt off.

And I gape at him. Shirtless Iain? I've never seen him do anything more salacious than exposing his calves when he wore his kilt. But now he sits there topless, and I get my first look at his muscular chest. Fine brown hairs pepper his skin. I want to trace the lines of his pecs and abs with my tongue, and the thought makes me suddenly feel warm and slick in places that are not appropriate right now.

Then Iain pulls on his new shirt, depriving me of the view of his gorgeous bod. But the fabric clings to his chest and biceps, which does not help me recover from seeing his naked torso.

"Fits just right," he says. "How did you know my size?"

"I guessed."

He glances at me sideways with a sneaky glint in his eyes. "Don't you want to try on your new shirt?"

A panicked laugh bursts out of me. "In your dreams, Dr. Mac-Taggart."

He wags his eyebrows, then winks. Starting up the engine, he pulls out onto the street. "Where should we go next?"

"I'm starving. Let's go eat."

"Aye, it is lunchtime."

We drive around for ten minutes until we spot a Mexican restaurant. Turns out we both love that kind of food. Who knew a small town in Wisconsin would have Mexican cuisine? But I'm glad we found this place. The food is amazing, and we have lots of fun talking while we share a bowl of queso. When the main course arrives, I devour my enchilada in a very unladylike fashion. Iain seems to think the way I eat is entertaining. Well, I am shoveling it in like I haven't tasted food in a month.

After devouring another loaded forkful, I wipe my mouth and give Iain a sheepish smile. "Sorry. I don't usually eat this way, but I am so hungry right now. Must be all that exercise we got while we were exploring the shops."

"Donnae care how you eat, sunshine. I like a woman who isn't afraid to show her passion for food."

Iain is the most unusual man of any age that I've ever met. I've never been the type to eat like a bird so I won't offend anyone, and I love that he appreciates my enthusiasm for food.

After lunch, we take a drive out of town to admire the scenery and the fields full of dairy cows. Iain teases me about my statement that cows are cute, and I respond by saying something that seems innocuous until the words come out. "Well, you and the cows have something in common. I think you're pretty cute too."

He jerks his head to look at me. Behind his sunglasses, I can't tell if his eyes are wide. But I think they must be. *Duh, Rae, you just flirted with him.* Accidentally, but yeah.

I swerve my attention to the windshield. "I just meant, um, that you, uh…"

"Relax, Rae. I know you didn't mean that the way it sounded."

Actually, I did. But I hadn't meant to say it out loud. "Maybe we should head back to town and my apartment. It's getting late, and I have homework to do."

"Let me buy you dinner first."

He's gazing out the windshield again, one hand on the steering wheel, seeming quite casual now. Guess the shock of my silly statement has worn off.

"I don't know, Iain."

"Please, Rae."

How can I say no to a sexy man who wants to buy me dinner? Other guys expect me to pay for my half of any meal. Of course, he might not have meant that he intends to pay for the whole thing.

"I want to treat you to dinner," he says. "You work hard, and you deserve it."

Wow. He does want to pay. "Okay. Thank you, Iain."

"My pleasure."

Oh, I wish he would never say that word again—unless he develops a squeaky voice. That smoky timbre coupled with his Scottish brogue makes me want to rip that T-shirt off his body.

How will I survive being friends with Iain?

Chapter Five

Iain

Two days ago, I treated Rae to dinner at an expensive restaurant. I hadn't known how pricey the food would be until I saw the menu, but I wasn't going to back out at the last minute. Rae deserves the best. She seems to take her studies too seriously, working harder than any student I've ever met. I have a feeling her home life might have something to do with that. But it's not my place to ask her about that, especially since I would feel obliged to explain what my life has been like.

I do not want to discuss that.

No, I would much rather enjoy spending as much time with her as I can. We're mates. Not…anything more. But I had noticed her expression when I removed my shirt in the car. She looked like a woman who wanted to do more than have a friendly conversation. *Bod an Donais*, I want to fuck her more than I've ever wanted to fuck any woman.

At least I won't see Rae as often this week. We finished her tutoring sessions at the museum, so I have no reasonable excuse for trying to see her again outside of class. All week, I avoid looking at her, though the fact she sits in the third row directly in front of my lectern doesn't help. Whenever she asks a question, I answer quickly and move on. I might be overcompensating. Never before have I become enamored of a student. But Rae is not an average undergraduate, and my feelings for her intensify every time I learn something new about the lass.

She eats with gusto. I love that. She gave me a silly T-shirt, and I love that too. Rae called me "pretty cute," and I even loved that. Aye, staying away from her seems like the safest option to prevent what I sense is coming.

If I keep seeing Rae, I will fall for her. Maybe I already have done.

After a week of trying to ignore the sweet lass, I go home and try to think of something, anything, I can do to take my mind off Rae. I could ring my parents, but I'm afraid of what I'll find out if I do. I love my father, but he has bad habits that I've had no luck talking him out of, no matter what I try. Bad habits? Aye, that's the polite term for it. He doesn't mean to do things he shouldn't, but he feels it's the only way to stay afloat.

So no, I won't ring my parents.

I can't do any work since I finalized all my lesson plans yesterday and graded all the papers then too. Maybe I could come up with some visual aids to accompany my lectures for next week. But making a slideshow doesn't take long, which leaves me with nothing to do but watch television. Cannae stand that for long. So I ring my cousin Lachlan, and we chat to each other for a while. He tells me humorous stories about what other MacTaggarts have done. Aye, we have an unusually large and unusually boisterous family. I miss them, but I love being here with Rae. *Mhac na galla.* I am not *with* Rae. Why can't I stop thinking about the lass?

By evening, I've had enough of struggling not to think about Rae. Maybe I can temper my desire for her in another way. Avoiding the lass hasn't worked. I need to take a radical approach. It's the only way I might get her out of my head. I will see Rae again on Monday, but by then, I'll have gotten this lust out of my system.

I step into the shower, turn on the water, and let the steam swirl around me. Then I shut my eyes and picture Rae. She's naked. Lying beneath me on a bed. I have no idea what her body looks like, but I have a vivid imagination when it comes to that bonnie, sexy lass. While I envision fucking her, complete with the sound effects of her moans and the wet slapping as our bodies collide, my cock begins to stiffen. I stroke it slowly while I switch my fantasy to something else. I imagine Rae kneeling before me, taking my length into her mouth, pumping me with one hand while she sucks and licks.

A deep groan rumbles out of me. I let my head fall back and keep one hand on the wall while I pump my iron-hard erection. Rae. Her mouth. My *slat*. Her soft lips enveloping me and her velvety tongue devouring me.

"Fuck," I groan while I pump faster.

Rae's mouth around me. Her erotic moans and grunts.

My body stiffens. I know I'll come soon, but I donnae want this fantasy to end yet. So I slap both palms on the wall and picture myself hoisting Rae off her knees to toss her onto the bed. She spreads her legs as if begging me to take her. I leap onto the bed and do what we both want, shagging the lass like a madman.

And my cock throbs.

I grasp my *slat* and pump it hard and fast, but I stop the second I feel like I might come. No, I'm still not ready for this to end yet. If I cannae shag Rae, I can at least pretend I've done it for as long as I can stand the pressure. It grows so intense that I cannae breathe, and my ears start to ring. I release my *slat* and slap my hands on the wall again, my fingers curling. My ears aren't ringing anymore, but I cannae catch my breath, and I feel like I my entire body might explode.

No more waiting.

While I picture myself fucking Rae so hard the mattress bounces, I grip my cock and pump it. The climax barrels down my spine so fast that I've barely finished my fantasy when I come, releasing everything I have while I shout and groan and finally sag against the wall.

Bloody hell. I've never experienced anything like that.

Have I slaked my lust for Rae? I sleep well that night. But my morning erection feels stiffer than usual, and I need to wank off again to relieve the pressure. Oh, aye, by the end of this semester, I will lose my mind for sure. Will I see Rae after the current class ends? She won't take another of my courses. Will she? If Rae does that, I might have a heart attack.

But I cannae stand the thought of not seeing her anymore.

I manage to arrive for my Friday morning classes without terrifying the students because my rock-hard *slat* finally cooperated with me, returning to a normal, family friendly state. I feel relatively normal as I set up the lectern and arrange my notes on it, then set up the projector and screen so I can share slides too.

Rae walks into the room and smiles at me. "Good morning, Iain."

And I drop the projector. It smacks down on the floor, scattering my slides. I hiss Gaelic curses under my breath as I struggle to reassemble things.

Rae kneels beside me to help.

I know she's trying to be helpful, but having her so close makes me flash back to what I did last night in the shower—while fantasizing about her. Now I'm staring at the lass as if she's just disrobed.

"Are you okay?" she asks as she hands me a disorganized pile of slides. "I can help you get the projector fixed."

"No, no, that's not necessary." I snatch the slides from her a wee bit too quickly, and her eyes flare wide. "Take your seat, Rae, please. I can deal with this."

"Well, if you're sure."

"Aye, I'm sure."

She rises but bends over to pick up a few slides that skidded under the lectern. And I'm staring at her erse which lies inches from my face. Just when I manage to tear my focus away from those cheeks, the lass turns toward me while still bent over and proffers the slides. "You missed these."

Now I'm staring at her tits, thanks to her blouse that sagged away from her chest.

I grab the slides. "Thank you. Now please go sit down."

Aye, I growled those words. Rae jerks her head back as if I surprised her, but then she rises and heads for her assigned seat. Thank the stars. If she had stayed in that position for much longer, I would've suffered a stroke.

The rest of the students begin to arrive, and I'm too busy fixing the slides to notice Rae anymore. I manage to teach the class without any further calamities and without gawping at Rae's body. I donnae know what's come over me. I never leer at women. I treat them with respect, which is what I need to do with Rae. She's no different from any other lass.

Of course she's different. I shouldn't deny that, but I also need to stop thinking of her in a sexual way. Aye, because it's so bloody easy to stop wanting a woman. We can be just mates, if I can get my lust under control. I had taught myself how to master my emotions and my desires, but moving to another country and starting a new job has thrown me off balance. Then I met Rae, and my Zen attitude flew out the windae.

All I need to do is recapture that state of mind.

That night, I meditate—my way. I don't do that "ohm" bollocks or try to turn my body into a pretzel. My version of Zen involves lying in bed, in the nude and with the sheets pulled back, while I shut my eyes and find my center. Maybe that is partially meditation. It's the Iain MacTaggart version. I often fall asleep while doing this, and tonight is no different.

I awaken in the morning feeling centered and calm, ready to face the day. But it's Saturday, so I have no classes to teach and no paperwork to tackle either. I feel bad about the way I snarled at Rae, so I decide to apologize to her. With my psyche centered and my cock once again cooperating, I dial Rae's number on my mobile.

She picks up on the second ring. "Iain?"

"Aye, it's me. How did you know?"

"I've got your number programmed into my phone, so it shows your name whenever you call."

"Oh, aye. That makes sense. I never think of doing that with my mobile."

She laughs, but it's affectionate and sweet. "You're kind of a Luddite, huh? It's cute."

"I'm not a Luddite. I just don't care about programming my mobile or playing games on it."

"Yeah, I'm not into games either. I get a headache from that stuff."

I clear my throat. "Rae, I'm sorry for the way I behaved yesterday."

"What did you do? I don't remember anything."

"Ye donnae remember me snarling at you?"

She hesitates, then laughs again. "Oh, that. I wasn't offended. You dropped all your slides, and anybody would get annoyed about that."

"Not me. I do not like feeling that way."

"Don't worry about it."

I shove my free hand into my hair and wince, though she can't see that. "Do you accept my apology, then?"

"Yes, Iain, I do. You are hereby forgiven."

"Thank you." I fidget in my chair, another thing she can't see. Thank heavens. "I wondered if you'd like to go sightseeing with me. I found something I think you'll appreciate since you love ancient history."

"Sure. Sounds like fun."

"I'll pick you up in an hour."

"Perfect." She hesitates again. "Um, how should I dress? Not knowing what kind of ancient thing it is, I'm not sure what clothes to wear."

"Dress for a casual walking hike."

She snorts as if she's trying not to laugh at me. "Casual walking hike? Is that a real thing? I thought people either walked or hiked. Never heard of doing both at once. Aren't those, like, the same thing?"

Fortunately, I had already reasserted my Zen attitude, so I'm not the least fashed by her teasing. "Dress for a walk, then."

"Gotcha. I'll be ready in an hour."

We say goodbye, and I change into appropriate clothes. As I head out the door, I realize I'm smiling. I always enjoy seeing Rae, but I am no longer in any danger of developing a problem that will expose my attraction to her. No, my *slat* will behave.

I whistle a tune as I climb into the car and keep on whistling during the drive to Rae's apartment building.

Chapter Six

Rae

When are you planning to tell me where we're going?" I ask. "I've had this blindfold over my eyes for at least ten minutes, thanks to your bossy command that I wear it because you 'cannae' trust me not to peek. I so do not appreciate that, by the way. I thought we were friends."

"Aye, we are." He pats my knee. "But I want this to be a surprise. And you were peeking. That's why I brought a handkerchief—so I could blindfold you in case you couldn't stop yourself."

"Hmm. I think you're full of it. I mean, you seem so calm most of the time, almost like the Buddha, but then you order me to get in the car and obey your commands."

"I never said that. And it wasn't an order. It was a fervent suggestion."

"Uh-huh." I want to roll my eyes, but he wouldn't be able to see that, so I don't bother. The sarcasm in my voice will accomplish the same thing. "If it's a suggestion, then I can take this blindfold off now, hey?"

"No, ye cannae."

Maybe I secretly love it when he gets bossy, and maybe I also secretly love all his Scottishisms and his accent and basically everything about him. But a girl needs to assert herself sometimes, just so the man she's with knows she is not a pushover.

Am I with Iain? Only in the sense that we're in the same car at the same time. It's not like we're dating. Friendship only. But more and more lately, I have trouble remembering that. We've never kissed or embraced, never even held hands, much less had sex. I want all of that, but I understand we can't go there. Iain only ever touches me in casual, chaste ways, like when he lays a hand on my back as we walk through a door. Occasionally, he touches my chin. But that doesn't feel romantic or sexual either. It seems more like a friendly gesture of affection.

I have so much affection for him. The crush I've had since the day we met has grown into something more. I still can't figure out exactly what it is. I know only that I love spending time with him and I feel so good when we're together.

The car begins to slow down. I know this because I can feel the gradual deceleration.

"All right," Iain says. "You can look now."

I whip the blindfold off and blink rapidly until my eyes adjust to the brightness of the sun. As Iain steers the car off the road and onto a paved driveway, I see a sign that explains where we are.

And I hop up and down in my seat while softly clapping. "Aztalan? Wow, Iain, this is amazing. I've heard of this place, but I've never had the chance to come here." I plant quick kisses on his cheek in between saying, "Thank you, thank you, thank you."

He chuckles while pulling the car into a parking space. "Don't think I've ever met another woman who gets excited about Pre-Columbian monuments."

"You know history is my thing. Of course I'm excited." I throw my door open and leap out, then lean in to grin at him. "Hurry up, Dr. MacTaggart."

He smiles and shakes his head, but he gets out of the car.

I race over to the historical marker, a brown sign held up by worn wooden posts, while Iain hurries to catch up. He stops beside me. I bounce on my toes as I read the words on the sign. "Wow, people lived here way before the Pilgrims set foot on this continent. How amazing is that? I've been to Cahokia, but this is my first time at Aztalan."

"Cahokia? I haven't heard of that place."

"Oh, it's really cool. Cahokia is in Illinois, right next to St. Louis. In fact, you can see the Gateway Arch from the top of Monks Mound."

"So, it's a mound site just like Aztalan."

"Yep."

He studies the sign, but I can tell he's pretending to read it because he keeps glancing at me furtively without moving his head. "Maybe we can visit Cahokia together sometime."

"I would love that."

We walk side by side across the parking lot and make our way toward the monument we came here to see—the rounded, rectangular mound backed by a strange-looking wooden barricade. The mound has two levels, each with an essentially flat surface, and stairs that lead up to the summit. The steps were probably added later to make it easier for tourists to ascend the mound. Iain and I stand here enjoying the panoramic view of the surroundings and the blue sky.

Since it's October, we both wore light jackets. I still feel a slight chill, though, thanks to a cool breeze. Stuffing my hands under my armpits doesn't help much.

Iain removes his leather jacket and drapes it over my shoulders. "You seemed a wee bit chilled."

"Thank you." I snuggle into the jacket. "You really are a gentleman, Iain."

"It's good manners, that's all."

While we explore the site, we chat about what life might have been like for the ancient people who lived here, and Iain suggests I might want to visit Scotland sometime to see the ancient cairns and standing stones there. I've learned about them in his class, but seeing those monuments in person would be incredible.

Especially if Iain served as my tour guide.

By the time we return to Nackington, I'm wiped out. Iain drops me off at my apartment building, and though he wants to walk me to my door, I tell him not to bother. He looks as tired as I feel. When he says "good night, sunshine" in that Scottish brogue, I want to crawl onto his lap and curl up to sleep there. Instead, I go into my apartment and barely manage to change into my nightie before I pass out on the bed.

I don't mind being exhausted when it happens because I spent an entire day with Iain.

The next morning, I'm sitting on the sofa with my laptop computer browsing information about Aztalan when my roommate finally emerges from her cocoon. It's ten thirty. But Cece yawns and stretches like she just crawled out of bed. I guess I'm the only college student who gets up before eight on weekends. Jeez, most of my fellow students don't get up that early on weekdays either, unless they have an eight o'clock class. Cece complains about having to go to class at ten.

My roomie drops onto the armchair across from me, propping her feet on the coffee table. "You're such a geek. Nobody gets up as early as you do, not during the week and definitely not on a weekend. But you do it so you can study."

Her lip curls faintly when she says the word study.

I love to learn. Even when I'm done with college, I will continue investigating everything that fascinates me. Cece will probably toss her diploma into the garbage can, then head for the nearest bar to get drunk. I don't hate her, but I can't understand the girl. She looks down her nose at everybody and skates by with a C plus GPA. I know that because she likes to brag about her GPA by saying "C plus means cool to the extreme."

"Good morning to you too, Cece." I close my laptop's lid and set it on the cushion beside me. "I made French toast, and there are leftovers if you want to eat it."

"Okay." She pushes up out of her chair and sashays toward the kitchen. "French toast is better than what you usually eat. Just looking at oatmeal makes me want to barf. I mean, that crap even looks like vomit."

Whenever she says snooty things, I ignore her.

My roomie gets a sneaky look on her face that matches her sneaky tone. "Sooo, who's the hottie you've been hanging out with? I saw you two in the parking lot last night."

I wish that statement surprised me, but it doesn't. Cece has turned out to be a nosy little snoop. "He's a professor at Nackington. We're friends."

"Mm-hm." She squints her eyes as she examines me. "Guys don't do the 'just friends' thing. He wants in your pants, and as soon as he's had his fun, he'll move on to the next girl."

Iain isn't like that, but I refuse to participate in this conversation any longer. So I open up my laptop and get back to work.

But she won't shut up. "I could have your professor anytime I want. Maybe I'll go for it."

Yeah, whatever. She's delusional if she thinks Iain wants to get in *her* pants.

Fortunately, she changes the subject.

"Halloween is on Thursday," Cece declares from the kitchen. I hear the microwave door click shut, then the thing revs up—to reheat the French toast, I'm sure. "Are you planning to stay home and study? Or will the geek come out of her shell to tap some hot ass?"

God, I hate it when she talks that way. It's so crude. "Not interested in dating. But I might dress up for fun."

"*You* are going to wear a costume?"

Does she have to sound totally shocked? I dressed up for last Halloween too, but Cece wasn't my roommate then. My old roomie transferred to Texas A&M over the summer, and I got stuck with Cece. Can't afford this apartment on my own. The university has on-campus housing, but it was all full too by the time my old roomie announced she was leaving.

Yeah, I never would've chosen Cece. She drives me nuts.

A few minutes later, Cece returns to the armchair with a plate of French toast drizzled with a dainty amount of syrup. I drown mine in the sticky stuff.

She sets her feet on the coffee table again and picks at her breakfast. "You're seriously going to dress up."

"Yep. I already rented a costume."

"Rent? Ew." She fake shudders. "That is so gross. Who knows who wore it before you."

"The costume shop dry cleans all their stuff before they rent it out again." I tuck my feet under me cross-legged. "What are you dressing up as?"

She slides a tiny piece of French toast between her lips and chews it like a bunny rabbit gnawing on a carrot. "My costume is totally hot. I'm going as Xena the Warrior Princess."

"Oh. That sounds…cool." I can't picture prissy little Cece wearing skimpy leather gear and pretending to be a warrior, but whatever. "I picked a historical costume. I'm going as Nefertiti."

"Nefer-titty?" Cece says with a snort of derisive laughter. "Can't picture you going topless to show off your titties."

"It's Nefer-tee-tee. She was an ancient Egyptian queen and one of the most beautiful women in history."

She snort-laughs again. "That's really not you."

I decide to ignore her and go back to browsing the internet for "nerdy" stuff about Pre-Columbian cultures. While I explore that world virtually, my mind starts to wander to other topics—like what I want to do once I graduate. I haven't thought much about that. I'm getting a degree in general studies, but I still haven't decided what to do after that. Maybe the upheaval in my family life has kept me from considering the future. But I suddenly realize exactly what I want—to go to grad school and study to be a teacher, a professor of English. Why do I want that? Well, maybe I want to work side-by-side with Iain. Maybe I want us to become an academic power couple. Does he even feel that way about me? I'm too much of a chicken to ask him about that, and I definitely can't ask whether he wants to kiss me.

By the time Halloween comes around, I've let that silly fantasy drift away into the recesses of my mind. I've got more immediate issues to deal with, like what Iain will think of my costume. I invited him to go to a Halloween bash with me, though not one on campus. We're going to a neighboring town where nobody will know us. I didn't tell Iain that was the reason. He thinks I just wanted to go to a more refined event than the ones hosted at Nackington University. Frat parties are so immature.

I put on my costume and look at myself in the full-length mirror attached to the back of my bedroom door. Will Iain like this? I can't wait to see what outfit he chose.

The doorbell rings.

Cece had left for a frat party an hour ago, so I rush out to answer the door. The second I swing it open, my jaw drops. Iain stands there, tall and proud and sexy as hell. He wears a kilt in what he had had once told his students is the MacTaggart clan tartan. But unlike the kilt he wore on the first day of class, this one consists of a single huge length of plaid wrapped around his hips and draped over his shoulder to hang down past his buttocks. A leather belt holds the whole ensemble in place. His *sgian dubh* sticks up out of his knee-high black socks, and black shoes cover his feet.

And oh yeah, he wears no shirt.

Seriously, *no shirt*. I'm gazing at his muscular chest—okay, I'm ogling his muscular chest and probably drooling too. Holy shit, he looks so good that I want to drag him into my bedroom and rip that plaid off his body. But I can't do that. *Rats.*

"Iain, you look amazing," I say, trying my damnedest not to drool or gawk at him anymore. "I love kilts, especially when you wear one."

He chuckles. "Thank you, lass. I love your costume too."

I tear my focus away from his chest and realize he's raking his gaze over my body with a look of hunger that I've never seen before from any man. His voice sounds rougher and deeper when he says, "You look every bit the Egyptian queen."

"I'm Nefertiti."

"Aye, that you are." He rubs his jaw as he drags his attention away from my cleavage to look me in the eye. "You are the most beautiful woman in history, for dead certain."

I'm wearing a white kilt-like pleated skirt that hugs my hips and thighs along with a bra that reveals more cleavage than I've ever shown before in public. My hat is modeled after the famous statue of Nefertiti, and a pleated white cape drapes over my shoulders. My high-heel sandals aren't exactly period appropriate, but neither is most of my outfit. This is Halloween. Who cares about historical accuracy?

The way Iain is devouring me with his gaze, I know he doesn't care about accuracy either.

Since we can't do what we're both thinking about right now, I clear my throat. "Should we go? Don't want to miss the party."

"Aye, we should go." He turns to the side and offers me his arm. "Allow me to escort the queen."

I can't help grinning. Iain makes me feel like royalty every time he looks at me. Am I in love with him? If I hadn't been before, I'm completely in love with him tonight.

Chapter Seven

Iain

loody hell. Rae looks so bonnie in her costume that I felt my cock rousing the moment I saw her. I can't seduce her. No matter how badly I want to feel her body enveloping my *slat*, I need to keep my lust in check. Tonight is for Rae. She wanted to go to a party, and I cannae deny her anything she desires.

Unless she wants to shag.

I don't care for parties, especially ones that involve costumes, but I find myself enjoying this do. A ceilidh is more my style, but no one in America has those as far as I know. I watch in awe as Rae charms everyone she meets, from students who traveled three hours from their university to come to this event, to elderly people and everyone in between. She doesn't behave this way at Nackington. I suppose she feels constrained there, and I've wondered if other students harass her about the time she spends with me.

Should I end our friendship? I have no idea what's right in this situation, but I know I can't give up Rae just yet. When she graduates… Donnae want to think about that.

I glance around to see where the lass has gone this time. To watch her having so much fun makes me smile, but I came here to spend time with her, not stand in a corner alone. Then I finally catch sight of her. She's on the dance floor taking a spin with an elderly gent, though calling it a "spin" seems inaccurate. The gent shuffles along with Rae. They both smile and laugh, and Rae positively glows. I wave until I catch her attention.

She says something to the old man, then kisses his cheek and sashays toward me.

The swaying of her hips mesmerizes me. I know this because she snaps her fingers in front of my face.

"Wake up, Iain," she says. "Did you drink too much wine?"

"No, I—" Rubbing my neck, I grimace. "I was distracted, that's all. And I didn't drink wine. I sipped Scotch, though it wasn't the authentic Scottish variety."

"Poor Iain. You can't get Scottish liquor in America."

"Are you ready to leave yet?"

She glances around, then her attention settles on me again. "Yeah, I'm done. This was a hoot, but I've hit my limit on revelry for the month."

I offer her my arm. "Allow me to escort you home, Your Highness."

Rae slips her arm around mine. "I feel bad for Nefertiti. She never got to be escorted back to her palace by a brawny Scottish warrior."

"That was a wee bit before the age of the kilt."

We exit the building and go straight to my car, which I'd parked directly across the street. As I help Rae into the passenger seat, she gazes up at me with a sweet expression. "If I could go back in time, I'd want to wind up in medieval Scotland. Kilts are hot."

She pulls the door shut.

And I stand here for a moment, frozen by what she said. *Kilts are hot.* She wasn't referring to me specifically, but I can't help wondering if she does think I'm "hot." Not that it matters. I can never be anything more than a mate to her. I drop Rae off at her flat, and I insist on walking her to the door. Though I experience a powerful impulse to kiss her cheek, I fight it. Even kissing her hand seems like too much. So I say good night and leave.

After Halloween, we go back to our usual routine of "hanging out," as Rae calls it. Neither of us discusses the party and what we both wore on that night. We're back to behaving like a professor and a student who have become good mates. It's bloody awful in some respects, but I'll take whatever time I can have with Rae. If she ever finds a boyfriend, I don't know what I'll do.

She told me once that she would be twenty-two in November, but I have no idea when her birthday is. I vaguely remember my faculty orientation, during which someone mentioned something about a Student Information System that I would have access to, though at the time I didn't see why I would want that. Now I need to use that system. No bloody clue how to do it. At some point, I was given a password that would let me "log in," but I'm not good with computers.

Time to expand my skills.

I get on my computer in my office and hunt about on the university servers until I find a link to the Student Information System. It takes me several more minutes to figure out how to log in to that, and even longer until I find the information about Rae. I can't see her grades except in my class, but I have no doubt she's doing as well in her other courses as she does in mine.

At last, I locate her birth date. She will turn twenty-two in eight days.

That's not much time to organize a celebration for her, but I can at least buy her some sort of present. Should I get a cake for her too? I can't bake. My mother attempted to teach me how to cook, but I failed so miserably at it that she told me never to try to cook or bake anything again. I've heeded her advice. I would need to buy a cake for Rae. What sort does she like? I can't find that information on the university server.

Since I'm a bloody-minded eejit, I embark on a campaign to trick her into revealing what sort of cake she prefers. This involves me asking sideways questions in the hopes I'll stumble onto the fact I need to know. Aye, I am most definitely an eejit. No one would go about this task the way I'm doing it.

The next day, as we sit on a concrete bench in the middle of campus, I begin my secret campaign. "Rae, do you enjoy sweets?"

"Sure. Doesn't everybody?"

"Not diabetics." What a dead stupid thing to say.

Rae laughs in the soft way she often does when I say something that's inadvertently amusing. "No, I guess they wouldn't. But yes, I love sweets."

"Do you eat them often?"

Now she seems a wee bit suspicious. "Often? I'm not sure. I don't keep a candy diary."

Of course she doesn't. I'm the worst interrogator on earth. A spy would know exactly how to get information. That's one of many reasons I should never become a secret agent.

What else can I do? I resort to the bull in a china shop approach. "I love cakes. Do you enjoy them?"

Rae freezes with a half-eaten sandwich hovering near her lips. "Uh, what?"

"I, well, asked if, ah…" I bow my head and blow out a breath, then raise my face to hers again. "What sort of cake do you like?"

She stares at me for a moment. Then the lass grins and punches me in the arm—gently. "Are you planning to buy me a birthday cake? I didn't realize you knew when my birthday was."

"Well, I…looked it up on the Student Information System."

"Ohhh. That does explain your bizarre fixation with sweets." She chews another bite of her sandwich before speaking again. "You don't need to do anything for my birthday."

"But I want to. I had the impression your family lives far away."

"Not that far away, but I doubt they'll show up to give me presents. My mom will probably send me something, though."

"Good. But I'd still like you to have a cake and at least one present. I'm incapable of baking, so this would be store bought."

She bites into a potato chip, chewing it slowly. "I'm not picky. I'll love anything you give me. You're very thoughtful and sweet."

"I don't think you should be alone on your birthday, that's all."

"Okay, but no present. Cake is enough." She leans toward me to whisper, "My favorite is chocolate with vanilla frosting and vanilla ice cream."

"I can manage that."

A laddie who is obviously a student, judging by his rucksack, walks right up to Rae, ignoring me. "Hey, I've seen you around campus. Wanna go out sometime?"

Rae's brows lift. She glances at me, but I remain calm, like the Buddha she thinks I am. So Rae turns to the laddie and says, "No thank you. It's rude to interrupt people who are having a conversation."

"Yeah, well, everybody knows about you two." He jerks his head toward me. "You shouldn't hang out with the Notorious Dr. MacT if you don't want everybody to think you're easy."

The laddie walks away before I get the chance to do anything. I want to hunt him down and batter the scunner for suggesting Rae is "easy." But that wouldn't fit with my Zen attitude, which Rae seems to like. Besides, that *cacan* isn't worth the trouble. Wee shits like him rarely are.

"Can you believe that?" Rae asks. "What a moron."

"Aye, he is an eejit for sure."

She bites her lip, which I've come to know means she's feeling shy about asking me something.

"Go on," I tell her. "You know you can tell me anything."

"Did you already know what the campus asses call you?"

"No. I had never heard that before."

She chews the inside of her cheek for a moment, but then rolls her shoulders back and looks straight at me. "That was the polite version of the nickname obnoxious frat boys invented for you." She squeezes her eyes shut, which makes her whole face pinch up. Then she says in a rush of syllables, "The full version is the Notorious Dr. MacT, Professor of Fuckology."

I say nothing for a few seconds. They call me what? Well, I suppose I should applaud the fact they used their brains for once to invent that nickname. After the shock wears off, I can't help chuckling. "That's quite a moniker they've given me."

"You aren't royally ticked about it?"

"Ah, lass, ye know me better than that. I never waste time letting scunners fash me. They aren't worth the effort."

"Right. You don't get angry. I mean, even that time when you growled at me, it didn't seem like genuine anger."

I snatch a potato chip from her lunch plate and chew it up before I can summon the nerve to tell her the truth. "I wasn't growling at you, not for the reason you think. You were, ah, bending over and your blouse fell away from your chest."

She clamps her lips between her teeth, and her whole body quivers.

Is she about to cry? "Rae, I didn't mean to upset you. Should've kept that to myself. I didnae mean—"

Rae bursts out laughing. "Relax, Iain, it's fine. I can see why that would 'fash' you. Sorry I accidentally exposed myself. You must've been so embarrassed."

"No, I wasn't."

We finish our lunch and go our separate ways. She hurries toward the science building while I make my way to my office in the humanities building so I can prepare for my next class. In the late afternoon, I endure office hours, which means listening to students complain, beg for better grades, or tell me their personal problems. I don't mind giving advice, but I know nothing about how young lads and lasses live these days. I grew up in a small town in the Highlands where everyone knows everyone else and we all poke our noses into each other's business. Most of those people are my relatives.

Sometimes I miss my home. But every time I feel melancholy, I think of Rae. Being with her erases all my homesickness.

The week goes by faster than I expected, but I made time to get everything for Rae's birthday. Though she doesn't want a gift, I can still make the day special for her in other ways. Rae deserves the best of everything. Since I don't want those annoying laddies on campus to blether about the two of us, I invite Rae to my apartment for a private birthday celebration. She orders me to promise I won't go overboard. Aye, I agreed to that. Anything for her.

I have everything set up by the time the doorbell rings.

Chapter Eight

Rae

The door swings open, and Iain smiles at me. "Happy birthday, *gràidh*. You look as bonnie as a sunny day, and I hope you're ready for a feast to celebrate your twenty-second year of lighting up the world with your presence."

"I thought we agreed you wouldn't go overboard." I have no idea what that strange word he said means, but I don't feel like asking him about it right now. "Everything you just said is the definition of 'overboard,' Iain."

"No. Unless I bring out a three-foot high cake and puppies burst out of it, I haven't gone too far."

"Puppies? I think it's strippers who jump out of cakes."

"Aye. But you wouldn't want that."

Maybe I'd like it if he jumped out of a cake and stripped for me. He'd be wearing his kilt and nothing else, then he'd unhook his belt and let that plaid drop. I've seen the man's chest twice, up close, and his brawny arms too. I can extrapolate from that what the rest of him might look like. Muscular chest equals muscular everything.

Iain steps aside. "Come in, Rae."

As soon as I cross the threshold, I can see what he's organized for me. It's nothing outlandish, nothing inappropriate, just the sweetest thing anyone has ever done for me. While Iain shuts the door, I hurry into the living room. The coffee table has been covered up with a blue cloth, and it now serves as a makeshift dining table. A cardboard box sits there alongside two plates hidden under dome-shaped lids, while two champagne flutes sit empty beside an unopened bottle.

This kind of seems like going overboard, but I won't chastise Iain for doing that. He could've really gone crazy. Instead, he held back and only went slightly too far. Besides, I love that he cares enough to create a beautiful birthday surprise for me.

"Sit down," he says as he enters the living room. "And enjoy the view."

My gaze shifts to the picture windows that bookend the glass doors to the balcony. His apartment isn't super spiffy or huge. It feels comfortable and just right for a man like Iain. Through the windows, I can see the lights of Nackington and the ghostly shapes of the hills beyond the city limits.

I settle onto the sofa, then Iain sits down a couple of feet away. "Thank you for doing all this. It's the sweetest thing any-one has ever done for me."

"You deserve it, Rae. I know how hard you work to get excellent grades, and I also know you're away from home like me. Maybe that's why I want to ensure you celebrate the little things, like your birthday."

My throat goes thick, and I feel a hint of tears stinging in my eyes. "You have no idea how much this means to me."

"Donnae cry. This is a happy occasion. Aye?"

I nod.

"Then let's enjoy your birthday together." He pulls the lids off the plates. "All your favorites."

Can't help giggling when I see what his grand meal con-sists of—fried chicken, French fries, mozzarella sticks, and ribs. Yeah, it's a strange combination, but I love it. When he opens the champagne and pours it into our flutes, I don't care that nobody eats fried chicken with champagne. Iain went to so much trouble for me, and I love him even more for doing that.

Not that I can ever tell him how much he means to me.

The food is yummy, but Iain feels the need to tell me he got it all from restaurants. Like I care. I want to kiss his cheek for being so thoughtful and honorable. Can't do it, though. Even in private, we need to maintain those damn boundaries to prevent us from getting into trouble. Once I graduate... No, I don't dare finish that thought. False hope will only make things worse.

After dinner, Iain clears the plates off the table and slides the big cardboard box into the center. "Now, for the pièce de résistance."

"Thought you were Scottish, not French."

"I'm trying to bring an elegant, continental tone to this evening's festivities."

"Uh-huh." I poke his arm. "Hope you're not violating our agreement about not going overboard."

"Not at all." He plucks up the cardboard box, revealing a cake seated on a platter. "Happy birthday, *sunshine*."

The cake has four layers of fluffy dark chocolate goodness sandwiched between vanilla frosting. The words "Happy Birthday, Rae" are elegantly scrawled across the top. I get choked up again and hold my hand to my mouth while I struggle not to cry.

"What's wrong, *gràidh*?" Iain asks. "Ye look miserable, but the cake was meant to make you smile."

"I'm not miserable. I'm happy." I spot a box of tissues on the end table and snatch one out of it, then dab at my eyes while sniffling. "This is just the most wonderful thing anyone has ever done for me."

He reaches out as if to touch me, but pulls his hand away. "Crying means you like it?"

"No. It means I love all of this."

"Oh." He scratches under his shirt collar and avoids looking at me. "Glad to hear it."

Have I embarrassed him? I thought the Unflappable Iain MacTaggart didn't experience discomfort of any kind. Well, he did get slightly flustered when I accidentally flashed him a glimpse of my cleavage. Other than that, he's always calm and level-headed. I often want to ask him how he manages to do that, but I don't have his equanimity. I'd get nervous and wind up saying something stupid.

Yeah, like "I love you, Iain."

Since I've never been in love before, maybe I don't really know what it feels like. I might have mistaken infatuation for love. He must not feel the way I do, anyway. He would've said something if he did. Right? God, I have no idea.

And now I've invented my own nickname for him. But I don't think I'll share it with Iain. It's goofy to call him unflappable.

Iain offers me a knife. "The birthday girl should cut the cake."

Cutting slices off a four-layer cake isn't as easy as it sounds, but I manage to get two pieces for us. Then Iain retrieves a carton of ice cream and dishes it out for us. We talk while we stuff our faces, mostly joking about the stupid boys on campus and the moronic nickname they gave Iain. Professor of Fuckology? What does that even mean? And Iain is the opposite of notorious. In the time I've known him, he has avoided causing a scene, no matter how often annoying jerks hit on me right in front of him.

Just the other day, a persistent twerp kept trying to flirt with me while I was sitting right next to Iain in the campus cafeteria. I told the idiot no three times, but he kept harassing me. Iain simply aimed his neutral expression at the boy and said in a placid tone, "You're interrupting our lunch, laddie."

The twerp threw his hands up and made a disgusted noise. "She's not worth the trouble, anyway."

And he walked away.

Did Iain's Buddha attitude scare that guy? I don't know, but I appreciate that Iain never gets upset.

I eat two slices of cake and more ice cream than I should have. Then it's time to go home. Iain walks me to the door, and we say good night. As I'm getting into my car, I notice Iain watching from his balcony. Only when I've pulled out onto the road does he retreat into his apartment. How many men would keep an eye out to make sure his guest gets safely on her way? Iain isn't like anyone else. Maybe that's why I have these strong and confusing feelings for him.

The weeks fly by after my birthday. Iain is busy getting ready for final exams and making sure all his students are prepared too. In the Celtic history class, he gives us half a dozen pop quizzes in the two weeks leading up to finals. Christmas is coming soon, which means I'll fly home to Iowa in ten days, then spend two weeks with Mom, returning to Nackington the day after New Year's. Being away from Iain for two weeks feels like ripping my own heart out, but I know that's silly.

Still, what I feel for him is not a simple crush. I know I love him, though I don't think I'll ever be able to tell him so. My only hope is that after graduation, he will tell me how he feels. If he says I'm just a "mate," that would destroy me. But I won't give up the months I have left with him. However our story goes, I will see it through until the end.

A few days before final exams, I get a surprise phone call at seven a.m., just as I'm getting ready to leave for the campus.

"Hello, Rae," a familiar voice says when I answer the call. "It's your father."

"Oh, hi, Dad. What's up?" I haven't heard from him in months. Not so much as an email. He didn't even send me a birthday card.

"Look, here's the deal." He sighs heavily. "Brooke and I are moving to Hong Kong so I can take over as general manager of the company's resort there. It's a major promotion."

"Um, congratulations?" I sound uncertain because I am. Totally confused might be a better description.

"I'm starting a new life with Brooke. Can't let the shadows of my past ruin the best thing that's ever happened to me." He pauses, then adds, "Don't try to contact me ever again. I hope you have a good life, but I can't be a part of it anymore."

He hangs up.

I hold the phone in front of my face and stare at it for I don't know how long. My father just disowned me. A chill races over my skin, sinking deep under the surface. I stagger to the sofa and drop onto it while still holding my cell phone. I've started to shiver, though I don't think it's from the cold air outside. Can't really think at all, though, so maybe the temperature has plummeted below zero, inside and out.

Cece sashays out of her bedroom and barely glances at me. "Morning, roomie. I'm heading out early for a breakfast date with a real steamy piece of ass."

What did she say? It sounded like gibberish to me. I can't do anything except stare out the window, not seeing anything. My dad told me never to contact him. He has a new family. With a woman two years older than I am.

Peripherally, I notice when Cece grabs her backpack and purse and heads for the door. "See ya later, roomie."

I stare blankly at the window for several minutes after she leaves. Then I rouse from my stupor enough that I know I need to do something. I can't go to my classes today. No way. But I don't want Iain to worry if I'm not there. So I clumsily call up his number on my phone and dial it.

"Rae?" he says when he picks up.

"Hi, um, yeah, it's me." My voice sounds a little shaky, but I can't seem to make it stop doing that. "I can't come to class today. I'm… sick. Sorry. I just need to—Well, I should rest. Okay?"

"Of course. Maybe you should see a doctor. Ye donnae sound well at all."

"Just need rest. I'm sure I'll be fine tomorrow. Goodbye."

I hang up, but my hands are shaking so much that I drop the phone. All I can do is stumble into the bedroom and curl up in a ball on top of the covers. Tears dribble down my cheeks. I don't sob. And I only cry for ten minutes, then I make myself get up and go into the bathroom to take a shower. Just as I'm getting dressed, the doorbell rings.

Scuffling to the door, I peer through the peephole.

Iain stands there, tall and gorgeous and wearing a calmly determined expression.

Oh God, I can't see him now. But I can't just tell him to go away either. So I open the door a few inches to peek out at him. "What are you doing here? Shouldn't you be teaching a class?"

"Aye. But I called in my teaching assistant, and he's handling my classes for today."

I rub my eyes, still feeling kind of off-kilter. "Why would you do that?"

"For you." He leans against the jamb. "I'm worried about you, *gràidh*. Please let me in."

"Um, okay." I scuffle backward so he can walk inside. Then I wave toward the living room. "Sit wherever you want."

He pushes the door shut and studies me. "Have you eaten anything this morning?"

"No, I don't think so."

"Ye don't think so?" He grasps my arm to lead me toward the sofa. "Sit down. I'll find something to feed you for breakfast."

I huddle on the sofa with my knees tucked up to my chest and my arms wrapped around them. Iain grabs a fleece throw and drapes it over my shoulders. Then he disappears into the kitchen. I blow my nose and go back to staring at nothing.

A few minutes later, Iain sits down beside me, holding a bowl and a glass of milk, both of which he offers to me. "Oatmeal. It's the only thing I know how to make. Please eat it, Rae."

I never can resist him when he asks me to do anything. So I take the bowl and start picking at the oatmeal. Iain holds the glass of milk, handing it to me whenever I ask for it, then taking it back so I don't have to try to balance that and my bowl on my lap. The more I eat, the better I feel. Or maybe I feel that way because Iain is here taking care of me. By the time I've finished eating, I'm not shaking anymore.

"Feeling better?" Iain asks as he brushes damp hair away from my face.

"Yeah, I feel a lot better. Thank you."

"Anything for you, *gràidh*." He wriggles until he's half-turned toward me and stretches an arm across the sofa's back behind me. "You are coming with me. We will have a good time, and you'll forget all about whatever made you so miserable this morning."

How Iain can issue a command and make it sound so calm and reasonable, I don't know. But my mood improves even more when he tells me that. I started feeling better gradually after he arrived, but now I can't help smiling, though not as much as usual.

"Does your smile mean you'll come with me?" he asks.

"Uh-huh. Where are we going?"

"To a museum. You love Egyptian antiquities."

I set my oatmeal bowl on the table. "We've seen all the Egyptian exhibits at the Nackington Museum."

He shakes his head, his lips curling into a slightly devious expression. "I'm not taking you there. Ye need a break from this town and the university. We're going to Milwaukee, to a museum that has a limited engagement exhibition of Egyptian antiquities. You'll get to see the golden mask of Tutankhamen."

"Really?" Yeah, now I sound excited. I leap to my knees and simultaneously spin toward him. "Tutankhamen's mask? What else?"

"You'll see, lass. You'll see."

Chapter Nine

Iain

Rae loves ancient history more than any student I've ever met, possibly more than any human being I've ever met. The bonnie lass races into the museum the moment I shut off the car's engine, and I need to sprint to catch up to her. She'd been distraught when I arrived at her flat, but her mood improved after she ate—and particularly after I informed her of my grand plan for the day. She's adorable when she gets excited about history. When I told her the exhibition also includes one mummy, she squealed with delight like a wee bairn.

Aye, then I wanted to kiss her. But I didn't do it.

She hadn't been unwell, not physically. That's all I know. Though I want to ask what made her so miserable, I know it's not my place to question her. If she wants to tell me, I'll listen. Since I have no desire to explain my family life to her, I cannae expect the lass to share all her secrets with me.

A few days later, after Rae finishes all her final exams, she gets on a plane headed for Iowa to visit her mother. Though I wanted to drive her to the airport, I realized that wouldn't be appropriate. Too often I've skirted the line between friendship and something more, blurring the distinction between student and professor. Having Rae as a mate might be the best thing that's ever happened to me, but I never want to overstep. She might not feel for me the way I feel for her.

Two weeks without her, without even speaking to her on the phone, tests my Zen attitude more than anything ever has. I could fly home to Scotland, and my mother wants me to do that, but I make up excuses why I can't. If my father gets into trouble again, I don't know if I can rescue him. I know he means well, but nicking things from strangers doesn't help anyone.

Staying here in Nackington without Rae… I have no words for how empty the whole world feels without her in my life. I know she will fly home the day after New Year's, but classes won't start again until the following day. She isn't my student anymore, so I might not see her at all. She doesn't need me anymore. Maybe she found a laddie her own age to, ah, be her…friend.

I'm sitting behind my desk in my office on campus, poring over the lesson plans I'd made over the past two weeks, when Rae stumbles into the room. Literally. She stumbles into a chair, almost knocking it over, her expression full of excitement. Her grin melts the ball of ice that had formed in my chest on the day she left. My pulse beats so fast that I feel almost lightheaded.

Though I want to rush over there and pull her into my arms, I force myself to stay in my chair and gaze at her with a neutral expression. "Are you all right, Rae? Have you hurt yourself?"

"No, I'm fine." She straightens and grins. "I got my grades for last semester. Straight A's. My perfect four-point-oh GPA is intact."

I cannae help myself. I jump out of my chair and hurry around the desk, reaching out as if to…hug her. But I freeze a few feet away from the lass. My face must look blank. When I finally regain my equilibrium, I clear my throat and do a dead stupid thing. I shake her hand. "Congratulations. I knew you would do well. You're the cleverest person I've ever met."

"Thank you, Iain. I loved your class, and I was hoping I'd get to have you again this semester."

Have me? Aye, I'd love to have her for certain. But I know she didn't mean it that way.

Now her face goes blank, though her eyes flare wide too. Mine hadn't done that. I think. She must've realized her statement sounded slightly inappropriate.

Rae hunches her shoulders and gives me a bashful smile. "Anyway, I couldn't get into any of your classes. Since you won't be my teacher anymore, I understand if you don't want to hang out with me."

"Rae, I want to spend time with you even if I'm not your teacher." I touch her arm. "We're mates, aren't we?"

"Yeah, of course."

I withdraw my hand. "Then nothing will change, except that I won't get to see your bonnie face in the classroom anymore."

"Learning about Scotland from you was amazing."

"Teaching you has been a privilege and a pleasure." I wave toward the door. "If you have time before your next class, we could have a celebratory dessert in the cafeteria."

"Sure, I'd love that."

After our sweet snack, I walk Rae to the science building. I pat her arm as we say goodbye, though I want to do much more than that. She seems vaguely disappointed. Even if she feels the way I do, we can never act on those desires. I might be imagining that she wants more. I don't have time to worry about that, though, because I need to hurry to get to my next class. A teacher's job is never done. When I reach the sidewalk, I pause to glance back.

Rae has just pulled the door open. She waves and gives me the sweetest, most beautiful smile. My chest aches, and I suddenly can't catch my breath. Even after Rae walks into the building, I stand here for a moment reveling in the afterglow of that smile. Even the snow on the ground can't lessen its warmth.

Aye, I'm in love with Rae Everhart.

If I'd thought not being her teacher would mean I see less of Rae, I was wrong. She visits my office sometimes, but only to ask me questions about Scottish history. We spend the most time together away from the campus when we take trips to nearby sites that have some relation to history, the older the better. By early February, we've seen most of the historical sites in Wisconsin.

Since I still feel that I need an excuse to spend time with her, so no one will think we're romantically involved, I keep coming up with reasons to invite her to my flat. I've only been to her apartment once. Maybe she doesn't want me there because of her roommate, or maybe she's uncomfortable with the idea because the only time I was there happened to be the day I found her in a state of shock. I don't mind if I never visit her apartment again, as long as I can see her.

What will I do when the semester ends and Rae graduates?

Valentine's Day sneaks up on me, and though I shouldn't care about that, I experience an irresistible impulse to give Rae a gift. Valentine's isn't only for lovers. Children give their friends and family cards, after all. I'm no bairn, but I want Rae to have something special for the holiday. A friendly gift. Nothing romantic. Luckily, I had brought something with me to America that I think she'll like.

I start to wonder if Rae has psychic powers when she finds me in my office and invites me to come to her flat on Valentine's Day for "pizza and pop." She seems genuinely surprised when I say yes, but her shock soon changes to excitement. I love how exuberant she can be when I surprise her with a road trip or just agreeing to eat pizza and pop with her.

On the night, I arrive precisely at seven o'clock, as she dictated. Aye, the lass can be bossy. I love that about her too. She's very bonnie when she orders me to do things. I have her present wrapped up in pink paper that has red hearts on it and with a pink bow on top. I know she loves that color. I ring the doorbell and wait.

She yanks the door open almost instantly, as if she'd been waiting for me. Rae smiles, then her gaze falls to the package in my hand. "You didn't need to bring anything."

"It's Valentine's Day." I thrust the present at her. "Friends can give each other gifts for this day. Aye?"

"Sure, yeah." She hugs the gift-wrapped package to her chest. "Thank you, Iain. Nobody has ever given me anything for Valentine's Day."

"Never? I should've bought you flowers too, then."

"Whatever you give me is plenty. But I should've gotten you something."

"No need."

I follow her into the apartment, and we both sit on the sofa—at opposite ends. I sat down first, and Rae opted to settle onto the cushion furthest from me. So I move over to sit in the middle, much closer to her.

"Open your present," I say. "It will complement your eyes."

She turns the package over several times as she studies it with the most adorable look of concentration. Her tongue pokes out between her lips, and her eyes glitter with excitement. She seems to relish drawing out the suspense, but I get impatient.

"Are ye planning to open it this year?" I ask. "Or not until next Valentine's?"

She flashes me a sly grin. "Maybe I'll wait until later."

"You're teasing me, aren't you?"

"Of course." She grasps the package and rips it open with both hands. The bow springs free and lands on my chest, held there by the adhesive strip attached to it. Rae laughs. "Look, the bow is right over your heart."

The same place where a piece of her will always live.

She extricates her gift from the remnants of the wrapping paper. Her eyes go wide. She lifts the scarf and gazes at me with what I can only describe as awe. "Iain, is this—It looks like the same fabric as your kilt."

"It is the same." I rest my arm on the sofa's back, my fingers grazing her shoulder. "It's the MacTaggart clan tartan. My mother made that scarf for me, and now I want you to have it."

"Me? Why?" She sets the scarf on my lap. "Won't your mother be upset you gave it away?"

"No." I hand the scarf back to her, and she fingers the fringe at either end. When she tries to give it back to me, I drape it around her neck. "Please accept this as a token of... friendship."

She bites her lip while she runs her hands up and down the soft plaid fabric. "Okay. I accept and appreciate your thoughtful gift."

"Good."

We enjoy the pizza and pop, though I have to ask for clarification about what that term means. Rae laughs and says, "Soda pop. You know, carbonated beverages." Aye, I would've guessed that, but being a newcomer in this country, I needed to make sure.

A few weeks later, the dean of the humanities department calls me into his office for a "conference." As soon as I sit down opposite his desk, he begins to interrogate me. Not what I expected.

"I've been hearing things about you," Dean Milton says. "Not good things, Dr. MacTaggart. How many students have you slept with?"

"None." And I don't appreciate his tone or the baseless accusation.

The dean leans forward, his arms locked on the desktop. "I've heard what everyone calls you. The Notorious Dr. MacT, Professor of—Well, you know the rest, I'm sure."

"It's not my fault juvenile laddies have decided to call me a moronic name."

He sighs and leans back in his chair, rubbing a hand over his eyes. "In my experience, rumors that spread do so for a reason."

"Aye. The reason is boredom and jealousy."

"What about Rae Everhart?"

I set one ankle on the other knee. "Donnae understand the question."

"Of course you do. What have you been doing with an undergraduate?"

"We're mates."

He jerks his head as if I've struck him, though I haven't come within three feet of the eejit. "Did you just admit to having sex with her?"

"Sex?" I chuckle. "No, sir, I did not confess to anything. I said we're mates. That means we are friends."

"In what language?"

"Have you never been to the UK?"

The dean's brows draw together as he studies me. "Of course I have. But you are Scottish, not British. Only people from England refer to friends as mates."

I can't stop myself from sighing. "Scotland is part of the UK. If you've been to England, you must know that."

"My travel habits are not the issue." He leans forward again, almost hunching over his desk. "I want to know how many students you have seduced."

"For the second time, the answer is none. I do not sleep with students."

Dean Milton stares at me for a moment while his expression tightens into something almost like pain. Then his face relaxes. "All right. I will accept your response—for now. But I'll have my eye on you, Dr. MacTaggart."

I don't bother to respond or even say goodbye. I march out of his office and shut the door behind me. Though I've tried to like Dean Milton, I failed at that. The best I can do is tolerate the weaselly man, thanks to his lack of a spine and his filthy insinuations. Let him think what he wants. I have never violated the university's ethics code.

The months roll by, but I hardly notice the passage of time. Why? Because Rae and I spend most of our free time with each other, visiting places of less historical value like a dairy farm and a museum dedicated to the sport of fishing. Rae enjoys those destinations, but she doesn't get as excited about them as she had done with Aztalan or the campus museum.

Before I know it, the semester is ending.

I'm sitting in my office grading final exams when Rae rushes into the room. She stands there for a moment breathing hard, apparently waiting to catch her breath. Even while she does that, she grins at me. Her lopsided expression makes me smile too.

"You seem excited," I say. "Have you found another barmy roadside attraction to visit?"

She shakes her head. "I finished all my final exams."

"I see."

"That means I'm technically not a student anymore. Just thought you might want to know."

My mouth opens, but I snap my jaw shut. My mind cannae quite process what she just said. Not technically a student. She finished her exams. The reality of what that means at last penetrates my brain, and my pulse races, every beat thundering in my ears.

Oh, aye, I know what she meant.

"I have a few things to take care of here," I say summoning all my Zen-like calmness to keep from leaping across the desk to drag her into my arms. "Go home, wait for me."

Rae's grin broadens. Then she whirls around and hurries out of my office.

Forty-two minutes later, I knock on the door to her flat.

The second it swings open, I surge across the threshold, pushing Rae inside. Then I back her into the door and push it shut, pressing my body to hers.

And I kiss her.

She straps her arms around my neck while I thrust my tongue into her mouth, groaning with the deepest satisfaction I've ever felt. I'm kissing Rae. Finally. She moans and rocks her hips into me while I explore her mouth with all the subtlety of a starved man who at last found a meal. She tastes like heaven, like everything sweet and savory and perfect.

When we peel our lips apart, I gaze straight into her eyes. "I need to make love to ye, Rae. But first, I want to give you the all the dates we never had—today."

"All in one day?"

I brush my lips over hers. "Aye, all in one day."

Chapter Ten

Rae

Iain kissed me. Wow. That kiss had taken my breath away and made me tingle from head to toe, especially between my thighs. He wants to make love to me. God, I want that too, so much. But I also love the idea of spending the day with him, as a couple, enjoying all the stuff we couldn't do before. This day is heaven.

Suddenly, I'm glad I researched how to give a blow job. Yeah, okay, that's weird and slightly deranged. But I wanted to make sure I'd know what to do if Iain and I ever had sex.

He insists on taking me to a lovely little café for breakfast, one we had never visited before. The place just opened up a few weeks ago, but I'd heard the French ambiance and cuisine are exquisite. The word of mouth didn't lie. Iain and I share a meal—literally, as in sharing one plate and feeding each other. I've never loved eating more than I do today, especially when Iain slides a French toast roll-up into my mouth.

But even the most delicious delicacy of all can't compare to the taste of Iain's kisses.

After breakfast, he whisks me away to a shopping mall where he insists on buying me whatever I want. I tell him I don't need anything, only him. He hits me with the steamiest smile I've ever seen, then rushes me into a photo booth. Never in my life had I stepped into one of these contraptions. I never saw the appeal of hunching inside a booth to take cheesy pictures of yourself. But today, I get it. With Iain, this doesn't seem like a dumb thing to do. It feels romantic.

Once we've squeezed into the booth, he slings an arm around me to tug me into his side. As the camera snaps pictures of us, we both grin and laugh as we press our cheeks against each other. I can't believe the Unflappable Iain MacTaggart is behaving like a lovestruck teenager, or that I'm doing the same. Everything about him today makes me feel exhilarated and free and so damn happy.

Just in time for that last picture, he pulls me close and kisses me.

As we peel our lips apart, he gives me a different kind of smile. The sweet kind, imbued with tenderness and something much deeper. Even if he never says the words, in this moment, I know he loves me as much as I love him.

Iain grabs the photo strip, handing it to me. "You should keep this, love. I don't need mementos to remember this day forever."

We stroll along the streets of Nackington, stopping in to explore all the cute little shops. Though we don't buy anything, shopping with Iain is even more fun than I remember from that day when I'd given him a silly T-shirt. Oh yeah, real men definitely wear plaid skirts. I would've loved it if he'd worn his kilt today, but that would've caused a distraction for every person we passed on the street. I don't want anything to mess up our day together.

After lunch, we go to a movie theater. Neither of us watches the movie. We sit in the back row and make out. The way Iain kisses makes me melt from the inside out, and I can't give up his lips until the movie ends and I have no choice but to ooze out of my seat while he leads me back to the car. He reclaims my lips the second we're in the vehicle, breaking away only long enough to drive to a smokily lit restaurant and order a sensual meal consisting of oysters, figs, spicy and savory delicacies, and a dessert of strawberries drenched in warm chocolate sauce with a hint of vanilla flavor.

I had no idea food could be so erotic. Maybe it's the sizzling-hot man feeding me who creates that steamy atmosphere, not the meal itself.

When we settle into the car, Iain takes possession of my mouth yet again, devouring me with a kiss of such intensity and sensuality that my heart pounds and my sex throbs. I know we will make love tonight. It's inevitable.

He drives to his apartment, and it takes us fifteen minutes to reach the second floor. We can't stop kissing. Iain even punches the stop button in the elevator so we can devour each other for even longer. I can hardly stand the anticipation. Even as we stumble out of the elevator, our lips remain fused. We stumble through the door to his apartment, stumble across the living room, and fall onto the sofa without ever giving up each other's mouths. We make out there on the cushions for half an hour.

But he still hasn't touched me in any overtly sexual way. Doesn't seduction involve a lot of fondling and sexy talk? Since I've only been with two guys in my entire life, I have no idea what to expect. But I'm beginning to worry that kissing is all he wants to do tonight. After ten months of holding back, I want everything with him.

I'll die if he doesn't make love to me tonight.

He pulls his mouth away, depriving me of the taste of his lips, and a frustrated noise grunts out of me. When I open my eyes, the look of unadulterated hunger on his face steals my breath and weakens my knees. Good thing I'm sitting down. Otherwise, I'd dissolve into a pool of molten lust at his feet. But beneath that hunger I see a tenderness that makes my throat go thick.

Iain combs his fingers through my hair as he traces circles on my cheek with his thumb. "Stay with me, Rae."

The smoky timbre of his voice makes me feel weak in the best way. "I'd love to."

His lips quiver the slightest bit as he gives me a soft yet carnal smile. Then he pushes his arms under my bottom and hoists me up while he springs off the sofa. Cradled in his strong arms, I can only gaze adoringly at his face like the lovestruck fool I am. This almost feels like a wedding night, with the groom carrying his bride across the threshold, except he isn't crossing the doorway of our new home. He's whisking me away to his bedroom for what I pray will be hours of intensely romantic and outrageously hot sex.

Based on our kissing, I know I'll get exactly what I want.

Iain sets me down near the foot of the bed. My knees wobble a teeny bit, but I'm not about to collapse. Before I can move a single muscle or form even half of a coherent thought, he begins to undress me, taking his time as he unhooks buttons, unzips my jeans, and removes every last stitch of my clothing while keeping his hands on my skin the entire time. The sensation of his palms skimming over my body arouses me even more, almost to the point of pain, because I've waited so damn long for this moment. Once I'm naked, he pulls the covers back and lays me down on the bed.

Then he slowly removes all his clothes.

Watching him unveil that body little by little… Holy shit, I might pass out from the power of my lust for this man. I'd seen his muscular chest before, but now I get to drink in the sight of his narrow hips and powerful thighs, though I can't resist studying every inch of his chest and biceps too. But it's his glorious cock that captures my focus so thoroughly that I can't stop staring at it. He is fully aroused right now. The long, veined length of his erection proves that all my fantasies over the past ten months fell woefully short of the reality. I want him inside me this minute. This second. I *need* it.

But I have no voice to tell him that.

He lies down beside me, skating his hands over me from head to toe with such leisure that I clench my fingers and bite down on my lower lip. This feels incredible, like a dozen feathers dancing over my skin, but when he touches his lips to my flesh, I can't stifle the soft whimper that rushes out of me. He retraces the path he'd taken with his hands, exploring me with his mouth, nibbling and licking as he travels over my body. By the time he reaches my throat, I'm panting and wriggling and so fucking wet that my cream drenches my sex and the hairs on my mound.

My other lovers hadn't wanted to go slow. Wham, bam, let's have a beer. That had been their method. But Iain seems in no hurry to get to the main event, as calm in bed as he is in the rest of his life.

Zen sex rocks.

His hair tickles my cheek as he flicks his tongue out to tease the corner of my mouth. Then he pulls my earlobe between his lips and suckles it so gently that I close my eyes to revel in the sensations he evokes in me. But when he shimmies down the bed to swallow my nipple, I clutch his head and arch my back.

"Iain, oh God, yes," I whisper as I force my eyes to open. Don't want to miss one second of the look on his face.

He slides his body over mine, holding himself up with both arms, then gradually lowers his full weight onto me. But he still doesn't penetrate my body. Instead, Iain kisses me tenderly while he glides his hands down my sides and back again, his touch delicate and maddeningly sensual. My nipples rasp against his firm chest as he spreads my thighs with his knee and pushes his cock inside me oh-so-slowly, filling me up inch by inch until I feel light-headed from the pleasure and the swiftness of my pulse. He pulls his hips back and plunges into me over and over, always maintaining a measured, gentle pace.

A groan rumbles out of him, resonating in his chest and vibrating against my nipples.

With his mouth still fused to mine, he closes a hand around my breast and begins to knead it in a leisurely, sensuous rhythm that has me clinging to his biceps and wanting to cry out, but I can't do that. His lips and tongue won't let me.

His other hand drifts down to my knee, and he slips his fingers between my thighs, dragging them up until he finds the slickness that coats the hairs on my mound. He gives up my mouth so he can rise onto all fours, his dick now dangling between our bodies. He lunges his head down to capture my nipple and pluck at the stiff peak with his teeth while his erection brushes across my belly, spreading my own wetness across my skin.

Though his need to come tightens his features and tautens every muscle in his body, he doesn't let go and fuck me like crazy. I'd love that, but somehow, the slowness and aching tenderness of the way he makes love to me feels more intense and pleasurable than anything I've experienced before. Not even the orgasms I gave myself while thinking about him can compare to this moment.

He lowers onto his elbows and shimmies his hips until his cock lies nestled between my folds. As gently as he has done everything else, he glides his length up and down my cleft, and I lose all control of myself, bucking my hips up into his movements in a desperate attempt to take him inside me. I grasp his shoulders to get more leverage, but still, he doesn't take me, not the way I want—with his hard, hot dick buried inside me. I moan and whimper, my nails digging into his flesh.

With a husky groan, he sinks his length into my body.

My hands fall down to his biceps, gripping him hard. I feel like I have no control over my muscles, as if an outside force has seized me. Though he keeps thrusting in a steady, even rhythm, I thrash and moan and shout things that aren't quite words, suddenly incoherent because of what he's doing to me. A high-tension wire inside me stretches tauter every second, until it chokes off my voice and freezes the breath in my lungs. The velvety hardness of his cock glides in and out, inflaming my already wet and achy flesh, and the sound of our bodies merging fills the room, a slick sucking that counts out the rhythm of our lovemaking, while the scent of my cream wafts around us.

I open my mouth but can't produce anything except a sharp gasp.

Without leaving my body, he rises to his knees and shoves his hands under my ass to lift it off the mattress. Still, he continues at that insanely hot and maddening pace that makes me want to both pull my hair out and beg him never to stop. That electric tension intensifies, and I feel myself crawling up a cliff, clawing my way toward orgasm, as my entire body goes rigid and Iain keeps thrusting. I fling my hands out to clamp them around the headboard rails, my mouth open, unable to breathe until...

The climax hits me so hard that a half-strangled scream explodes out of me. My inner muscles pulsate around his cock, making him hiss in a sharp breath. Even while my orgasm goes on and on, he doesn't speed up at all, plunging inside me and pulling out again over and over and over until his face cinches up with the best kind of agony—and he comes.

"Fuck, Rae," he growls, thrusting a few more times. He holds the last thrust as if his body has turned to stone. Even his expression doesn't change. I swear he's not breathing either. Just as I'm about to smack his cheek to wake him up, he exhales a long, groaning sigh that relaxes every muscle. He pulls out and lies down beside me with that Buddha smile on his lips. "Worth the wait, aye?"

"Oh, yeah. So worth it." I reach for the covers, but he bats my hand away. "What are you doing?"

"We are not done yet." He lays a hand on my thigh and skims it up and down my skin. "But before we have another go, I need to feed you."

"Not hungry. We had dinner already."

He smiles with so much heat that the expression could melt an iceberg. "I want to feed ye sweet, sensual treats to bolster ye for another shag."

"Oh. Well, go ahead and do that."

I watch him slide off the bed and saunter out of the room, admiring his tight ass and those strong thighs until he moves out of sight. I felt all his muscles tonight. Sex with Iain MacTaggart blew away all my expectations. And now, we have the rest of our lives to revel in the afterglow together.

Chapter Eleven

Iain

I return to the bedroom holding a bowl of ice cream. Rae lifts her brows when she notices me, but she doesn't say anything. Her attention swiftly shifts to my body as she roves her gaze over me, and her lips curl into an expression of appreciation and hunger—not for food, though. I know she craves my body as much as I crave hers. After ten months of fighting my desire for Rae, I needed all my Zen willpower to keep from ravishing her like an animal.

Rae is beautiful after a shag. I love the way her cheeks and chest have been dappled with a rosy pink. Her lips still seem slightly swollen, but they've looked like that for most of the day. Neither of us wanted to stop kissing. We had to, of course, in order to eat and drink and use the bathroom. And while I was driving. But we are not in a car right now. And I've come up with a way to kiss her and feed her at the same time.

She licks her lips as I sit down on the bed beside her, but I can't decide if she hungers for the ice cream or me. I allow myself a moment to drink in the vision of her nude body one more time, then I slap her hip. "Sit up, *gràidh*. Cannae feed ye when you're lying down."

Rae shimmies backward while pushing up with her arms until she can lean against the headboard. "I'm ready. For anything."

"I already knew that." I slide closer to her and dive my spoon into the ice cream. "I brought you two sauces for this treat—hot fudge and caramel."

She rubs her palms together, and her tongue pokes out between her lips. "Yum. But there's only one spoon. Are we sharing?"

"The spoon? No."

I turn partway toward her and pull the spoon out while fudge and caramel drizzle over its edges to coat the ice cream. Then I slide the spoon into my mouth.

"Hey!" She kicks my foot. "Thought we were sharing."

Smiling with my lips sealed, I lean toward her and press my mouth to hers. She opens for me without hesitation, the way she's done all day, and I deepen the kiss to mingle the taste of her with the flavor of the ice cream, fudge, and caramel. *Bod an Donais*, those flavors drive me mad. I haven't tasted *her* cream yet, but I mean to do that soon.

We explore each other's mouths for several minutes while I keep slipping bigger and bigger spoonfuls of our dessert into my mouth before I dive in again to devour her. She moans and thrusts her tongue deep as if she means to take all her nourishment from me. I would love that, but this was only foreplay, or maybe intermission. I haven't fulfilled all my plans for her body yet.

Still, I need to tease her a wee bit more. "Lie down again, please."

The lass doesn't even ask why. She slides down the bed until her head rests on the pillow, then raises her arms to clasp her hands near the headboard. The sexy slant to her smile lets me know she wants another shag as much as I do.

I fill the spoon with the melted remnants of our ice cream and drizzle it over her belly. Then I scoop up the last of the thick liquid and drop it onto her stiff nipples.

"Whatever you're doing," she says in a breathless tone, "keep doing it. Please."

"Aye, love, I will."

I bend over to lick the melted ice cream off her belly, starting near her navel and working my way up toward her breasts. Rae arches her back as a wee moan escapes her lips. She has the most beautiful body on earth, and I love the way she responds to my touch. I mean to keep giving her pleasure for the rest of our lives because I plan on proposing to her tomorrow. I need a ring first.

But right now, I need to make her so desperate for me that she'll say "Iain, oh God, yes" again.

When I flick my tongue over her ice cream covered nipple, she lets out a sharp cry. I swirl my tongue around that peak, delicately, again and again until she starts clenching the pillow and making desperate noises. Once I've licked all the ice cream off that nipple, I move to the other one and repeat the process.

Rae thrashes beneath me. "Oh God, Iain, please."

That's not the exact phrase she said earlier, but I love this one just as much.

Now that we've finished off the ice cream, I crawl down the bed to kneel between her feet. "Time for *my* dessert. I've waited a long time to feast on you, Rae."

"I've dreamed about this. About you…"

"Going down on you and lapping up every last bit of your cream?"

"Yes, oh, yes. I've wanted this for so damn long."

I chuckle. "Relax, love, I'm about to make your dream come true." I wink. "Multiple times."

She spreads her legs, and her chest rises and falls as she struggles to keep breathing evenly. She cannae do it, though. The lass is a wee bit excited about this.

I lie down between her legs and crawl forward until my face hovers above her mound. The scent of her desire envelops me, sweet and musky, more addictive than any drug. I rest my hands on her hips and dive in, lapping at her flesh and groaning as I get my first taste of her. It's as sweet as her scent, but even more intoxicating, but with a hint of saltiness. She bends her knees slightly while I drag my tongue up and down her folds, forcing myself to go slow and make this last—not only for her, but for me too. How had I stayed sane for all those months when I couldn't let on how much I want her? For Rae, I would endure any hardship to get to this moment with her.

She moves her hips in a circular motion, her breaths growing shallower and shorter. Could she already be on the edge? Given her reactions when I took her body earlier, I doubt she'll last long now. I imagine college laddies don't know how to give a woman real pleasure. The ones I've met at Nackington seem like the sort who would go off prematurely and leave the lass unsatisfied.

Why am I thinking about those scunners?

I focus on Rae, plunging my tongue inside her entrance while I tease her clit with my fingers, making her gasp.

"Oh, Iain, you're so amazingly good at doing—oh—this kind of—" She lets out a whimpering cry. "You're a god, Iain."

Her statement makes me sputter because I'm trying not to laugh while I have my tongue inside her. But that results in Rae thrashing again. I guess she likes what I accidentally did. So I lift my head and smirk at her. "Did ye like my new and entirely original method for driving you wild?"

She nudges my cheek with her knee. "Are you going to make me come sometime this year?"

Her sly smile assures me she is not annoyed.

I move my mouth up her cleft, taking my time so I can torment her flesh with soft kisses and fast flicks of my tongue. She makes a noise that's somewhere between a moan and a whimper with a slight gasp underneath. Every little cry makes my cock throb, but I donnae care. Once my lips close around her clit, I reach down to push one finger inside her. My gaze remains focused on Rae, on her expression and the way she bites her lip every time I plunge my finger into her body. But when I slide two fingers into her slick heat while devouring her taut nub, she shouts my name and her entire body jerks.

Her breathing has turned into sharp gasps.

Bod an Donais. The look on her face does me in, and I plunge three fingers inside her, pumping hard and fast, while I scrape my teeth over her nub and suckle it fiercely. She thrashes even more wildly, then her body stiffens. The moment her orgasm strikes, her muscles begin milking my fingers and strangled cries erupt from her.

"Iain!" she shouts as the final spasms wane. Then she goes limp, her bonnie tits heaving. "Wow, oh God, wow."

Rising to my knees, I lean forward to kiss her. "Say 'wow' again. It's dead sexy."

"Mm, wow." She sounds almost dreamy now, and her expression matches her tone. "You really are a god, Iain."

"A god?" I say with a chuckle. "No. I'm only a man."

"Not to me. You're…" She fans her face with one hand. "I can't even describe how amazing you are."

"Let's find out together." I kneel between her legs again, and she spreads them for me. On hands and knees, I straddle her body. "One more time before we're both too jeeked to go again."

She seems puzzled, but she doesn't ask me what "jeeked" means. Tomorrow, I'll explain all the things I've said to her—and I'll start with *gràidh*. It means "darling." Then I'll call her *mo chridhe* and tell her that means "my heart." She is that for certain. Maybe I'm too old for her, but I don't care.

Soon, I'll need to tell her about my family—and my father. But not tonight.

I slide into her like I donnae care how long this takes, going slow so I can experience every sensation. The slickness of her cream. The satiny smoothness of her body molding to my cock. The way her hairs tickle my *bagais*. I lower onto my elbows and press my lips to hers while keeping my eyes open. She keeps hers open too, and we gaze into each other's eyes even as I plunge inside her again and again. She grips my biceps, her soft gasps in rhythm with my thrusts.

I love you, Rae, I want to say. But I cannae speak.

So I seal mouth over hers and let her blue eyes hypnotize me while I thrust faster and deeper, suddenly unable to catch my breath. The pressure builds inside me until I cannae breathe at all, cannae move except to keep punching into her. My ears ring, and I feel like I'll explode any second.

I throw my head back as my harsh yell echoes in the room and I come, spilling everything deep inside her body, the sweet pressure finally released. Nothing else has ever felt as satisfying as making love to Rae. I hold still for a moment, unable to move even to lie down beside her. The warmth of her sheath surrounds my cock, and I'm breathing so hard that I cannae speak.

Rae combs her fingers through my hair. Her loving smile gives me a pang in my chest.

When I finally pull out of her body, I lie on my side and cradle her to me. "Are ye happy, love?"

"Never been happier." She makes a pained face. "But I need to pee."

I slap her erse. "Go on. I think I can survive a few minutes without you. But no more than that."

She kisses me, then hops off the bed and trots into the bathroom.

Rolling onto my back, I gaze up at the ceiling and imagine what our life together will be like. Rae mentioned the other day that she wants to become a teacher and she's applied to graduate schools. Whatever she wants to do, I know she'll excel at it.

A yawn overtakes me, and I fold my hands over my belly, shutting my eyes. I imagine us going to work together, teaching together, doing everything together. We'll have bairns, and they will all be bonnie, clever lasses like their mother.

I drift off to sleep with that dream in my mind.

Chapter Twelve

Rae

Iain had fallen asleep by the time I got done in the bathroom last night. Well, we did have sex twice. I've never done that before, but I can believe it would make a man wiped out and in need of serious sleep. So I didn't disturb him. I crawled back into bed and pulled the covers over us both, then cuddled up to Iain. I fell asleep not long after that.

This morning, I wake up sprawled over Iain's body. My arm is draped across his torso, my leg is draped over his thigh, and my cheek rests on his chest. I can hear his heart going *thump-thump, thump-thump*. I rub my cheek over his skin, inhaling a deep draft of Iain-scented air because he smells unbelievably good. Like sweat and sex and pure man.

His hand rests on my bottom.

I never did get around to showing Iain what I'd learned about blow jobs, but I don't care. Last night was incredible.

Iain sighs and grasps my ass. *"Guten Morgen, mein Liebling.* About bloody time ye woke up."

He's speaking German again. I have no idea what the second part means, and right now, I don't care.

"Good morning, Iain." I can't resist gliding my hand down his chest to his groin and laying my hand over his slowly growing erection. "Could we, um, do it again right now?"

He chuckles. "Later, *gràidh*. First, we both need a good breakfast to fortify us." He squeezes my ass. "Donnae worry. We have all the time in the world, and we will shag again later."

"Promise?"

"Yes, love, I promise." He kisses my forehead. "Are ye sore at all?"

"Only a little."

"Well, then we definitely should wait until later to have another poke."

I roll onto my back and exhale a long, satisfied breath. Then I stretch and sit up, gazing down at the gorgeously nude Scotsman lying beside me. I want to do nothing but admire his body all day long.

But Iain sits up too. "Let's get dressed."

I make an annoyed noise. "Can't we stay in bed for a few more hours?"

He shakes his head, though he's smiling. "If we do that, I'll shag you again. Ye need time to recover first."

Reluctantly, I get out of bed and put on the clothes I'd worn yesterday. I don't have anything else to wear since this isn't my apartment. Will Iain want to move in together? God, I hope so. I want to spend the rest of my life with him.

Iain makes oatmeal for breakfast like he had on that day in December when I'd been miserable. Yeah, I don't mind at all that he sucks at cooking. He makes up for that one flaw with all his amazing strengths and talents. After we eat, he drives me back to my apartment. I open the door and turn to face him on the threshold.

"Wait for me here," he says. "I have a few last things to do at my office. Shouldn't take more than an hour or two. Then we're both free for the summer."

"Free to do any damn thing we want."

His smile warms me up from the inside out. "Aye, whatever we want."

Iain kisses me and walks away.

Shutting the door, I close my eyes and lean back against it. A smile tightens my lips. The man I love wants to be with me. Life is perfect.

"What do you think you're doing?"

The angry voice of my former roommate snaps me out of my reverie. I push away from the door. "Cece? You don't live here anymore. You left yesterday."

"Yeah, but I forgot my favorite pair of undies in the bathroom." She stalks up to me, her features twisted into the nastiest expression I've ever seen. Her voice is just as nasty when she shoves me into the door and says, "You fucking slut!"

"What's your problem?"

"You." She stabs her finger into my chest so hard that I wince. "What right do you have to screw a teacher? I knew your sweet little girl act was bullshit. You just couldn't wait to get your skanky hands all over him, could you?"

"My what?" I can't understand anything she's saying. Why should she care if I'm dating Iain? As far as I know, she's never met him.

Cece steps closer, leaving only a few inches between us, and spittle sprays onto my face when she starts ranting again. "You are the dumbest geek on the planet. Do you seriously think the hot professor wants to see you again?" She huffs and rolls her eyes. "News flash. He only wanted to have some fun and play out his sugar daddy fantasy."

Then she really goes off, cursing at me in the vilest, most infantile way imaginable. I barely pay attention to her tirade, so stunned that I can't move or speak. I've never done a thing to Cece, yet she has apparently despised me with a vengeance for the whole ten months I've known the girl.

"Of course the teacher wanted to get some," she snarls. "Guys will hump anything with a vagina. Only a stupid piece of shit like you would think it means something."

Cece glowers at me for a few seconds, then she whirls around and storms into the bedroom she used to sleep in.

I slump against the door and struggle to make sense of what just happened. She called me horrible names because I did what? She assumes I slept with Iain, which I absolutely did, but I have no idea why she's so enraged about that. Cece has a boyfriend. That girl definitely has loose screws inside her deceptively pretty head. Maybe an entire dump truck full of them.

I can hear Cece in her room shouting at someone—or maybe just railing at the injustice of me dating Iain. Who the hell knows? The girl is crazy. Ten minutes go by before she falls silent. A moment later, she stalks out of the apartment, never even glancing at me. She slams the door hard.

Ohhh-kay. I'm elated that I'll never need to see that nutjob again. After all, she mentioned several times over the past ten months that she's moving to New York City to study at a "prestigious school of design." At least Cece the nutjob is out of my life for good.

Hallelujah.

Since I have to wait for Iain, I go into my bedroom to pack up my stuff. In addition to my suitcases, I kept the cardboard boxes I'd used to mail my other belongings to this apartment. While I do that mindless task, I start to worry about what Mom might think about me and Iain. I mean, he's closer to her age than mine. Will she freak when she learns that her daughter is shacking up with a man fifteen years older? I shouldn't worry about that yet. Mom isn't expecting me to come home until the end of the week, which gives me time to figure out how to break the news. Today, I just want to enjoy the best thing that's ever happened to me. I love Iain MacTaggart. I know he loves me too, though neither of us has spoken those words. We will today. I'll say it first if he hesitates. Guys can be silly about emotional stuff.

Once I finish packing, I carry the suitcases and boxes into the living room, setting them down beside the door. Iain can help me carry them out to his car or my car when he gets back from the campus.

I feel different this morning. Not because of the hot sex we had last night. No, I feel different because I finally found something good. My dad might've destroyed my faith in men, but Iain has shown me that not all of them are jerks. He is wonderful.

With nothing else to do until Iain comes back, I watch TV and eat junk food.

Hours go by. At noon, I try to call Iain on his cell. No answer. When it goes to voice mail, I hang up. I try his office number too, but get no answer there either. What if he had a car accident? I pace the width of the living room for another ten minutes, then try both his numbers again. My heart is racing, I'm chewing on my lip, and I feel nauseous. So this time when his voice mail picks up, I leave a message.

"Iain? It's Rae. Um, you said you'd be back in an hour or two, but it's been four hours. Are you okay? Please call me. I'm really starting to freak out. I know I'm probably being silly, but please, just call me back? Okay?"

After hanging up, I realize how stupid and desperate that sounded. I can't help that. Iain always does what he says he'll do. If he promised to come back in an hour or two, he would do that. So I call every hospital within sixty miles of Nackington. But I still can't find him. I want to call my mom, but what could she do? Nothing. I'm an adult, and I can handle this on my own.

Five minutes after twelve noon, I jump into my car and race to Iain's apartment. My pulse pounds so hard and fast that I feel almost faint. But I will not pass out. Iain must be in some kind of trouble, and I will not stop until I find him. I trip when I burst out of the elevator, catching myself just shy of hitting the floor, and sprint to the door of his apartment. I ring the bell over and over, then give up and start pounding my fists on the door.

"Iain! Are you in there? Iain!"

A door across the hall opens. "Is something wrong, dear?"

Whirling around, I see an elderly woman gazing at me with concern. Tears burn in my eyes, ready to pour down my cheeks any second. I swallow hard, but my lip trembles and my voice comes out shaky. "Um, yeah, something is wrong. Do you know the man who lives in this apartment? His name is Iain MacTaggart. I was supposed to meet him today, but I can't find him anywhere."

"Oh, you poor dear." The woman walks over to pat my arm. "Are you his girl? Iain is such a nice man. He always carries my groceries for me."

"Have you seen him today?" I choked on the last word, and the first tears trickle down my cheeks. I sniffle and say, "I'm so worried about him."

"I can see that. Have you called the police?"

"N-no. But I think I should check his office before I do that."

The sweet woman pats my arm again. "You do that, dear. I'm sure you'll find him and realize everything is fine."

"Uh-huh. Thank you. I'm so sorry for bothering you."

I sprint to the elevator and tap my toes on the floor while the car descends, though it feels like it takes an hour to reach the ground floor. Ten minutes later, I'm sprinting across the campus and into the humanities building. The door to Iain's office hangs open. He must be in there, right? He locks the door every day when he leaves.

But I stumble to a halt when I reach the threshold. The desk is empty. Like no one has ever used it. I stand here breathing so hard that my ears ring.

Footsteps approach in the hallway, stopping just behind me. "Uh, miss?"

I spin around, almost falling over in the process, and gape at the janitor standing on the threshold. "Where is Iain MacTaggart? This is his office."

"Not anymore." He winces. "Sorry. I heard he quit or got fired or something. Anyway, they told me he's gone. I was supposed to clear out this office and then lock up. Just finished cleaning, then I almost forgot the locking-up part."

My brain can't form words. My voice won't function either. All I can do is shuffle past the janitor and shuffle down the hallway. I push the doors open and walk back to the student parking lot in a haze of confusion and numbness. Everything from my skin down to my bones seems to have turned to ice.

Back in my apartment, I sit on the sofa staring at the wall. After a while, I pick up the phone, intending to call the airline and move my flight up to tomorrow. But I stop myself before I even finish dialing the number. I need to get away from here, but I can't leave yet. When my mom calls to get the details about my upcoming flight, I recite the information in a voice that sounds eerily calm, even to me. Mom doesn't seem to notice. After we say goodbye, I go into my room and curl up on the bed, on my side, hugging my knees. And I let the tears flow.

Iain, where are you?

Chapter Thirteen

Iain

Leaving Rae feels like cutting my own heart out. But that's rubbish. I'll see her in a few hours, once I've done what I need to do and closed out my office for the summer. I'm not teaching again until the fall. If Rae gets accepted to a graduate school somewhere else, I'll go with her and find another position for myself. All I care about is being with her. The rest we can work out together, as a couple.

My first task takes me to a jewelry store.

Aye, I mean to make Rae my wife. Donnae care about our age difference. I've never loved anyone else and I never will. As I browse the glass cases, hunting for the perfect ring, I can't help imagining what our life together will be like. Will Rae's mother accept me? She might think I'm too old for her daughter, but I will do whatever it takes to ease her worries and prove that I will care for her daughter and cherish Rae forever.

I've become a lovestruck fool, and I donnae give a damn.

"This one," I tell the store clerk, pointing at the ring I want.

It isn't large, but it's not too small either. I doubt Rae would want an enormous stone since she doesn't like me to "go overboard." The clerk rings up the purchase and puts the ring in a velvet box. Though he offers to give me a bag for it, I decide to keep the box in my pocket instead. On my way back to the campus, I stop at a flower shop to buy a bouquet for Rae. White roses. I think she'll like that. Red seemed too severe for a lass who exudes light and life from every pore on her body. Aye, I'm completely off my head, but in a good way. The final tasks I need to complete shouldn't take long, which means I can rush back to Rae soon and ask that all-important question.

As I approach my office, I have my head down, gazing at the flowers in my hand. Though I hear scuffling sounds up ahead, the fact they're coming from my office doesn't register in my mind until I walk through the door and nearly crash into someone.

Raising my head, I freeze.

Three security guards are inside the room. Two of them seem to have just finished dumping all my files and everything on my desk into bin bags. I see my name plate sticking out of one bag.

"What's this?" I ask.

The men turn toward me, all of them looking stern. One bloke aims a flinty glare at me, while the other keeps his hand on his holstered gun and taps one finger on it. The third seems more relaxed, at least in his posture, and he gazes at me with a faintly pinched expression.

"Come with us, please," the guard with the flinty glare says. "The president wants to see you."

I doubt he means the President of the United States. "Why? I was just about to leave for summer break."

The gun-tapping guard twists one side of his mouth into a sneer. "You aren't going anywhere except to the president's office."

I glance at my empty desk, and a prickly sensation rushes over my skin, raising the hairs on my arms.

A guard snatches the bouquet from my hand, flinging it into a rubbish bin.

The other two guards each seize one of my arms and force me to walk with them down the hall. The third guard follows, maintaining a short distance behind us as if they think I might try to escape. Am I a prisoner? It certainly seems that way. But why? I have no idea.

We march outside and straight across the quad to another building, the one that houses various offices, including that of the university president. I'm so dangerous that I require three guards to control me? *Mhac na galla.* Even as we walk into the building and step into an elevator, the two guards maintain their grip on my arms. The third stands in front of us now. Everything becomes a blur while we trudge out of the elevator and down the fourth floor hall to a doorway identified as the "Office of the President."

But when we enter the room, President Schaech isn't the only person there. Dean Milton from the humanities department also waits inside, as does Conrad Bremner-Ashton, the university's single largest donor and the father of Rae's roommate. All I know about Conrad is the rumors that have percolated through the campus, most thanks to the wagging tongues of students. The gossip suggests the Bremner-Ashtons have been a sort of mini mafia that controls the town of Nackington and the university that bears its name.

I never believed that rubbish. But faced with the three powerful men in this office, I begin to wonder. Still, I shouldn't jump to conclusions since I don't know why I've been summoned here.

President Schaech sits behind his large desk, of course, while Conrad and Dean Milton relax in chairs on this side of the desk. An empty seat lies between them.

Schaech waves toward that seat. "Have a seat, Dr. MacTaggart."

I do what he suggested, and now I'm sandwiched between the dean and Conrad Bremner-Ashton. "What is this about? My office has been cleaned out with everything tossed into bin bags."

"Bin bags?" Schaech's brows draw together. "I guess you mean garbage bags. Yes, I ordered your office to be cleaned out since you are no longer an employee of Nackington University."

"What? I know the school year ended, but I have until July to decide if I want to extend my contract for another year."

"Request denied."

"I still don't understand what's happening. Just last month, you told me how pleased you've been with the success of my Celtic history course."

Schaech's expression has hardened, and he stares at me with a strange coldness in his gaze. "Conrad has told me what you've done, what sort of reprobate you are. I had no choice but to terminate your employment immediately."

"What do you claim I've done?" He can't know I slept with Rae last night. Besides, that's not illegal or an ethics violation.

The president looks at Conrad. "Why don't you do the honors? Explain the situation to this miscreant."

Conrad Bremner-Ashton turns slightly in his chair to face me. A smug smile tugs at his lips. "You seduced one student and sexually harassed another. That is a clear violation of the university ethics code."

"Bollocks. I never did any of that. Who told you those lies?"

He nods to one of the guards, who steps out into the hall. When he returns a moment later, Cecelia Bremner-Ashton shuffles over to her father and feigns being terrified as she glances at me. Her act is far from convincing. Cece should never try to become an actress because she's ruddy awful at it. No tears accompany her hiccuping wee sobs, and her eyes do not glisten with unshed tears. They aren't red either, as they would be if she had cried earlier. No, her eyes are clear and bright and glittering with excitement. Even her quivering lip is sheer artifice. Her mouth keeps shifting into a smile as smug as her father's, though she tries her best to hide it.

"Ye cannae believe this one-woman show," I say to Schaech. "She is lying."

He ignores me and stares down at his lap, clearly waiting for the real man in charge to speak.

"My daughter does not lie," Conrad says. "She can provide details concerning how you sexually harassed her in an attempt to seduce her into your bed."

"I donnae even like the cow. Why on earth would I want to shag her? This is pure rubbish."

Conrad lifts one brow. "Students call you the Notorious Dr. MacT, Professor of Fuckology. No one receives a nickname like that without just cause."

"You're using a moronic nickname as an excuse to sack me? College laddies make up things like that. It's how they entertain themselves."

"Stop talking, Dr. MacTaggart." Conrad leans toward me, his expression so full of hatred that I know he will never see reason. "You didn't only harass my daughter. You lured another student into becoming your illicit lover."

"I never touched your daughter, Conrad."

His lips curl into a sneer. "I'm talking about Rae Everhart."

All I can do is gawp at the man. How does he know I slept with Rae? My gaze gravitates to Cece, who has now given up her pathetic act and smiles with a smugness that tells me everything I need to know. She and her father have conspired to rob me of my position at Nackington. I don't give a toss about that. But if they do anything to hurt Rae…

"She's not a student," I say. "Anything I might have done with Rae happened after the semester ended. Ask her."

"We don't need to," Conrad says. "We have an eyewitness."

He looks up at Cece.

She lifts her chin and gazes down at me with supreme satisfaction. "I saw the two of you kissing this morning. I saw Rae go into your apartment last night too."

"You followed me?"

"I was worried about my roomie," she says in a tone of mock sincerity. "A lech was putting the moves on sweet little Rae, so I had to do something." She folds her arms over her chest. "Neither of you left that apartment until morning."

"So what? We are adults."

Every rumor I'd ever heard about the Bremner-Ashtons floods into my mind, and I realize how foolish I've been. The signs were there. Cece disliked Rae and was clearly jealous of her. Being a kind-hearted lass, Rae assumed the girl meant no harm. But the witch knew exactly what she was doing. Her obsession with the relationship between me and Rae had become far more intense than either of us realized. Now we are both in the crosshairs of a powerful family.

Conrad jabs a finger into the air near my face, almost grazing my nose. "You have two choices. Stay and fight, knowing you will be destroyed in the process. Or leave the country now."

"Leave the country? You're off yer head."

"Go willingly, or you will be deported by force. Unless you get on a plane today, we will punish your lover."

Bile surges into my throat, but I gulp it down. "Punish her in what way?"

"Any way we want."

I know from his tone and his expression that he means it. He will do who knows what to Rae, just to punish me for loving her and refusing to abandon the lass. I never even told her I love her. My mind races, but I cannae catch even a single thought, much less devise a plan in the next thirty seconds that might save me and Rae.

"You have until the count of five," Conrad says, "to agree to leave the country. Five, four—"

What else can I do? Rae's safety means more to me than my own life.

"Three, two—"

"I'll go," I say. Honestly, I have no bloody clue if they can have me deported, but I can't take that risk. "You've won, Conrad. I will leave the country."

Maybe I'm a sodding coward. I can't think clearly enough to know what the right thing is in this situation. *Protect Rae.* That's my only coherent thought.

Conrad straightens, his lips forming a nasty smile. "I'm glad you've seen reason. Your possessions will be shipped to you."

As I let the guards herd me out of the building and to a police car parked along the curb, I feel like I must've fallen asleep and this is all a terrible nightmare. Any moment, I'll wake up to find Rae lying beside me, her soft, warm body snuggled up to mine. But I will never see her again. She will never know how I feel about her. Conrad Bremner-Ashton has wielded all his power to rip us apart.

Two officers from the Nackington Campus Police Department escort me to my apartment so I can pack two small bags. They won't let me use the landline phone, and they confiscate my mobile, all so I can't contact Rae. Then they take me to the nearest international airport. I briefly consider running away, since the guards can't follow me into the terminal, but that would be a futile effort. As the wheels lift off the runway, I sag in my uncomfortable airline seat and cover my eyes with my hands. Cannae breathe. Cannae think. Donnae know what the fuck I'll do now.

But the memory of that beautiful night with Rae will stay with me for the rest of my life.

Chapter Fourteen

Rae

For three days, I scour the university and the whole town of Nack-ington in search of any sign of Iain. No one knows where he went, when he left, or why he disappeared. My tears have dried, and I've developed a strangely determined attitude that must come across as tough, because everybody seems kind of uncomfortable talking to me.

After days of searching, I'm exhausted. So I sleep for twelve hours, then I gather my bags and get ready for my departure later today. I'd already shipped all the boxes of my stuff to Iowa. My few bags look so lonely in the empty apartment.

I'm about to call a taxi to go to a restaurant for breakfast, since I sold my car yesterday, when the dean of the humanities department calls me. He says he urgently needs to see me in his office. My flight doesn't leave until this afternoon, so I have time to find out what Dean Milton wants. When I walk into his office, he tells me to shut the door and have a seat. Yeah, that doesn't sound ominous at all. His somber tone does nothing to quell the acid roiling in my gut.

I settle into a hard wooden chair.

"You must be wondering why I summoned you," he says. "I'm afraid it's not good news."

A chill shivers through me. Bad news? Is it about Iain?

Dean Milton clasps his hands on his desk and frowns down at them. "I've received disturbing information about you and Iain MacTaggart."

"What do you mean?"

He sighs heavily, then lifts his head to aim a stony expression at me. "I know you had a sexual relationship with Dr. MacTaggart while you were a student in his class on Celtic history."

"No, that's not true." I didn't sleep with him until after the semester ended. "Who told you that?"

"Cecelia Bremner-Ashton."

Oh, that goddamn bitch. Spreading lies? I knew she was a jerk, but this…

"The trustees met to discuss the issue this week, and they've reached a decision." He stares straight into my eyes, his gaze cold and unforgiving. "Your grade for that course has been changed to an F. This means you are one credit short of graduating. Since you're also being expelled, you will not have the opportunity to make up that credit. Your degree is null and void."

"What?" I almost whisper that single syllable, too stunned to say anything else. Expelled? That can't be. "But you're doing this based on a lie. Cece has been jealous of me, and she—"

"Stop right there. Blaming Cece will not spare you. The decision has been made, and no appeal is possible." He rises from his chair to peer down at me. "Goodbye, Miss Everhart."

I'd heard rumors over the past four years, gossip about the Bremner-Ashton family being like a Midwest mafia, controlling this town and the university. I hadn't believed it. The stories sounded too outlandish. But here, today, in the dean's office, I suddenly realize it was all true.

"You could hire a lawyer," Dean Milton says. "But I don't imagine someone like you could afford the fees. The Bremner-Ashtons will sue if you make any public comment about Cece or your expulsion."

He's right. I can't afford a lawyer, and even if I sold everything I own, I would never win the battle. When a powerful family wants you dead, metaphorically, they will get their way at any cost.

Dean Milton waves toward the door. "Leave now, please. By the way, you are also barred from setting foot on campus ever again."

Like I would ever want to come back here. Everything I dreamed of has been shattered into a million pieces.

As I'm walking out the door, Dean Milton tells me, "You should know the truth. Iain MacTaggart left the country of his own volition. He won't come back."

I swallow hard, but the constriction in my throat refuses to let up. Iain abandoned me. Maybe I shouldn't believe everything the dean told me, since he thinks my former roommate is a reliable source. But I can't imagine why Iain would have left of his own volition. He could've fought—for us, for me, for what I believed we had together. But maybe it was all a lie.

With no other options, I fly home to Iowa.

My mom picks me up at the curb just outside the airport terminal. I still feel weirdly calm and determined to do…something. Mom tries to engage me in conversation during the drive to our house, but I just stare out the window. Why did Iain leave? Did he do it voluntarily? The only involuntary way I can think of would be kidnapping. But that doesn't seem plausible. I mean, no one could have a reason to abduct a Scottish college teacher.

Who is Iain MacTaggart? Did I ever really know him? We never talked about our families. I know his full name is Iain Malcolm MacTaggart and that he grew up in Scotland, but that's about it. Maybe the fact that he never shared more about his past should've been a warning sign, but then, I'd never told him much about my past. Would we have shared everything on that fateful morning after he finished closing up his office? I never even got to tell him how I feel, how much I love him.

And I have no clue if he felt the same way.

We have all the time in the world, Iain had told me on the morning after our one and only night together. But we didn't have even the whole day. He walked out of my apartment and out of my life with no explanations.

Now I sit in the kitchen with my mom, staring down into a cup of tea while absently stirring it with a spoon and watching the milk swirl round and round. Just days ago, I was lying in bed with Iain. We were making love and sharing ice cream. Now he's gone.

Mom curls her hand around mine to stop my incessant stirring. "Please talk to me, Rae. What happened? Why are you so distraught?"

"Doesn't matter anymore."

"Of course it does."

I push the tea mug away, having drunk exactly none of it, and lean back in my chair to hug myself.

Mom watches me with a worried expression. "I wish you would tell me what happened, sweetie."

"Not today, Mom, please." Tears pool in my eyes, and try as I might, I can't stop them from spilling down my cheeks. "I don't know what happened, anyway. My life is over, that's all I know."

I drop my arms onto the tabletop and let my head fall down too as the tears become sobs.

Mom lays a hand on my back, rubbing it in gentle circles.

When I finally stop crying, she doesn't quiz me about what happened. She just leads me upstairs to the bedroom where I'd slept for my entire life, except for the time I was at Nackington. Over the summers, I slept here too. This is my home, but it doesn't feel that way anymore. No, I found a new home with a wonderful man.

And then it all came crashing down.

The next morning, I tell my mother everything. Well, almost everything. I can't bring myself to relate the events of that night with Iain. But I won't lie about the rest. "I fell in love, Mom. I met an amazing man who made me feel like we could conquer the world together. Iain MacTaggart is from Scotland, but he came to Nackington University last fall. I took one of his classes, and we became friends."

She doesn't speak. Mom just listens and watches me.

"We couldn't date because he was my teacher. But we both knew what we felt was more than friendship. Still, Iain behaved like a gentleman the whole time. Then my roommate got jealous and…" I squeeze my eyes shut for a moment. "She started a chain reaction that destroyed my life. I didn't just lose Iain. I lost everything I'd worked for, and I can't get it back. I was expelled."

"Oh, honey." She clasps my hand. "I know it seems like the world has ended, but you'll recover from this. One thing I know about my daughter is that she never gives up."

"I loved him, Mom." I tiny sob hiccups out of me as tears flow again. "I loved him so much."

"Oh, baby, I know."

"Maybe I misunderstood, and he didn't feel that way about me. I mean, why would a thirty-seven-year-old professor want to date a college senior?"

"He's how old?" Surprise flashes on her face, but only for a second. Then she regains her calm demeanor. "This man, this Iain MacTaggart, is fifteen years older than you."

I nod.

She puckers her lips, but she doesn't say anything. I can tell she doesn't approve of our age difference. It hardly matters now. Unless I can find Iain, I will never know how he really felt about me.

For weeks and weeks, I do nothing but wallow in my shock and grief. I'd never been in love until I met Iain, so I have no idea how to deal with the loss. Mom wants to help, but I just can't make myself talk about it anymore. Though I feel like I should get a job or something, every time I suggest that, Mom tells me not to worry about it. I have the rest of my life to figure things out, she says. Since I was expelled from Nackington, I don't know if I can get into another school to finish my degree. Do I even want that anymore?

Soon, two months have gone by—and I come to a realization that changes everything.

I've been feeling off for a while, but I assumed the tiredness and intermittent nausea was a side effect of grief. Then one day, I realize I haven't had my period since I left Nackington. No, I can't be—No. I rack my brain for information about that night with Iain and struggle to remember whether we used protection. I have no idea. The only thing I can recall for certain is the way Iain made love to me.

Later that day, I go grocery shopping with Mom. While she heads for the meat section, I tell her I need to go to the restroom, but what I really do is hurry to the pharmacy inside the grocery store and buy a pregnancy test. I stuff it into my purse to make sure Mom won't see. Until I know for sure, I don't want to worry her.

The next morning, I finally work up the nerve to take the test. The stick turns blue.

I'm still sitting on the toilet, with the lid down, and I let the test stick tumble from my fingers. Then I drop my head into my raised hands. I'm pregnant. In seven months, I will have Iain's child. *Oh God*. How can I do this without him?

The time for wallowing is over. I need to think about my child now. And that means I need to tell my mom the news. I find her in the kitchen making pancakes for breakfast. "Uh, Mom, can we talk?"

"Sure, honey." She slides the last pancake off the griddle and sets it on the plate with the others. Then she settles onto a chair at the table. "The look on your face tells me we should sit down for this."

"Yeah." I perch on the chair beside hers and just say it. "I'm pregnant, Mom."

Her face goes blank. She doesn't even blink. After a moment, she finally speaks. "Pregnant?"

"Yes."

She clears her throat and shakes off her shock. "The father is Iain MacTaggart."

I nod.

"But you have no idea where he is."

"No. Even if I never find him, I want this baby."

She grasps my hand firmly. "Of course you do. And I will help in whatever way I can. Have you been to a doctor to confirm it?"

"I did a home test. But I'll make an appointment today."

"Don't worry, baby. You can do this. Everhart woman always rise to a challenge and overcome adversity."

Mom has definitely done that. Despite Dad's cheating, despite the impending divorce, despite Dad running away to Hong Kong, she persevered. I couldn't ask for a better role model. So I lay my palm over hers, where she still grasps my other hand. "You're amazing, Mom."

In the afternoon, I go to my doctor's appointment and get confirmation. Yes, I'm pregnant. I don't need a doctor to tell me who the father is. The news spurs me to embark on a mission to find Iain, though I have no idea where to start. I try everything I can think of to track him down. Mom lets me do that and doesn't tell me I'm wasting my time, though she gets a disapproving look on her face whenever she catches me scouring the internet for men called Iain MacTaggart. Who knew there would be so many of those in Scotland? Iain never told me exactly where he lived, not even the general region. Scotland might be way smaller than the United States, but hunting for a specific Scotsman turns into the most grueling task I've ever undertaken.

But I will not wipe myself out in the process. I have someone else's life to worry about, and my child matters more to me than anything else. I'm not even showing yet, but I already love this baby more than I ever could have imagined I might. I can't resist closing my eyes every night before I go to sleep just to lie here and imagine what my son or daughter will be like. Iain is in those fantasies too, right there by my side.

As my search continues, I consider hiring a private investigator, but I don't have enough money for that. I can't ask my mom. She's been my rock ever since I came home and fell into a puddle of misery, despite the fact that she clearly disapproves of my relationship with Iain and the way I'm desperately searching for him. I tried to call his cell phone again the day after he disappeared, but I got a message that the number is no longer in service. Probably because it was a US number. When he went back to Scotland, he must've gotten a new one. When I resort to calling Iain MacTaggarts in the desperate hope I'll find the one I need, my mom puts her foot down. Yeah, the international phone charges might bankrupt me if I keep going.

"Stop this, Rae," my mom tells me. She's leaning over the back of my chair, where I sit with my computer on the desk in front of me. "You can't live like this anymore. I know you loved that man, but it's time to move on—for the sake of your child, if not for yourself. It isn't healthy to cling to something you can never get back."

I tip my head back to look at her upside-down face. "Sorry. I know I've gotten kind of obsessed. But you're right, it's time to lay that ghost to rest."

A few days later, when I finally unpack all my boxes that I'd shipped home from Nackington, I discover something that nearly does me in. I find the scarf Iain gave me, the one made from the MacTaggart clan tartan. My hands start to shake as I hold the fabric to my cheek, and tears dribble down to drip off my chin. I want to wrap that scarf around me and never take it off, but I can't dwell on the past anymore. I have a future to write for myself and my baby.

So I tuck the scarf into the back of a dresser drawer and get on with my life.

Will I ever forget about Iain? As much as I want to banish the ghost of him, I know our child will bind me to him forever, whether or not he ever learns the truth.

Chapter Fifteen

Iain

A mature man should know how to handle losing a lass, but I've lost more than Rae. I have no job and no prospects for finding another one because that bastard Conrad Bremner-Ashton has made certain of that. I am, for all intents and purposes, universally blacklisted. Dean Milton and President Schaech must have helped Conrad do that by spreading lies about me. I doubt he has the international connections to manage it on his own. What can I do now? Nothing. What will I do? Well, that's another question, one I can answer. As much as I wish I could say I've behaved like a mature man in the aftermath of the worst disaster I've ever experienced, I won't lie to myself. Certainly can't lie to anyone else either. Everyone witnesses my downfall.

Maybe if shagging half the women in the village of Loch Fairbairn had been my only mistake, I could've recovered from it better. But no, I doubt anything would've stopped me from sliding down that slippery slope into self-destruction. I never knew I had it in me. I wish I still didn't know. Learning the dark truths about myself does nothing to stave off the grief and shame of what I did to Rae, abandoning her because I was too cowardly to defy the Nackington mafia. Why didn't I fight for Rae? After I came home, I could have rung her to explain and to beg her to move to Scotland to marry me. I have no bloody clue if she would've done that. But I didn't even try.

The day after I returned to my homeland, I finally think to check the voice mail on my mobile. I can't do that, though, because the Nackington mafia had confiscated it, and now my service has been disconnected. It was a mobile I'd bought in America, anyway, so it might not even work over here.

Then I receive an email from Conrad Bremner-Ashton. The bastard has sent me an audio file with no text to explain what it might be. Maybe I shouldn't do it, but I open the audio file anyway.

"Iain? It's Rae. Um, you said you'd be back in an hour or two, but it's been four hours. Are you okay? Please call me. I'm really starting to freak out. I know I'm probably being silly, but please, just call me back? Okay?"

The fear and pain in her voice wrecks me, and I do something I haven't done since I was a wee laddie. I slump to the floor, bury my face in my hands, and cry.

After an hour, I wipe my eyes and get up. For three weeks after that, I try to pretend I'm fine, though I know I'm nothing close to it. Channeling my Zen side works for a while and convinces everyone except me. But not for long. I try drinking to numb the pain, but after a string of incidents at local pubs in which I behave like a *tolla-thon* and start brawls with laddies I don't even know, I realize I don't want to make a name for myself as a drunken ersehole. Then I turn to sex for pain relief. Shagging women in pub hallways and the backs of cars does little to alleviate the ache in my chest, though. No one else can fill the hole carved out of my heart. Only Rae can do that, but I've given her up.

Fate has a wicked sense of humor, as it turns out. Or maybe I'm just cursed.

I'm sitting in the living room of the house I rented last week since I didn't want to burden my parents anymore with my behavior. I've just turned on the television to watch a rugby match when my landline rings. The second I say hello, my mother sobs, "Iain, please come home now."

"What is it, Ma?"

"Your da, he—" She lets out another, harder sob. "Angus has been arrested again."

I jerk forward. "Arrested? For what?"

"The usual. We donnae have much in the bank account, and you know how Angus gets when the purse strings are tight. I know he does it because he loves me and wants to protect me, but I cannae go through this again. What if he's sent back to prison?"

Bloody hell. I thought we'd gotten past all that. "What has he stolen this time?"

"Donnae be angry, Iain. Your da doesnae mean to get into trouble."

Aye, he never does mean to do these things. I love my father, but I can't handle this right now. Doesn't matter if I can or not, though. I must deal with it. "Who did he burgle?"

"Rhys Kendrick."

"Who? I've never heard of the bloke."

"He's a Welshman who moved to Loch Fairbairn while you were away in America. Kendrick is very wealthy, apparently from mines that he owned and then sold." Ma pauses, and I can hear her sniffling. "Everyone knows Kendrick has a collection of... What do you call them? Some sort of trinkets."

"It must be worth a great deal for him to be arrested, which means it's no trinket."

"Aye, but I donnae know what it is. Something made of gold, I think. It's all so confusing."

"Relax, Ma. I'll take care of things."

Ten minutes later, I jump into the old Land Rover I'd bought recently and race to the police station in Loch Fairbairn. My father has indeed been arrested and charged with theft by housebreaking for stealing a solid gold bowl. Aye, that qualifies as a "trinket." Who the bloody hell needs a thing like that? The officers let me speak to my father, and he tells me what happened, which gives me the information I need to understand the situation. I leave him and head for the home of Rhys Kendrick.

A woman in a maid's uniform answers the door. "May I help you?"

"My name is Iain MacTaggart. I need to speak to Rhys Kendrick."

Her expression turns puzzled. "MacTaggart? You can't be the man who broke in and stole Mr. Kendrick's bowl."

"That was my father."

"Oh, I see." The woman steps aside. "Please come in. I'll let Mr. Kendrick know you're here."

I walk inside, and she closes the door. Then the woman leaves me in the entryway of this mansion while she wanders off—to find her employer, presumably.

Footfalls clap from elsewhere in the house. A large brute of a man veers into the entryway, his expression fierce and sullen. He halts an arm's length from me. "You dare to set foot in my house? The son of the bastard who invaded my home and stole from me."

"Aye, I dare to set foot. I'd like to discuss the matter with you, Mr. Kendrick."

"Discuss?" His lip curls into a nasty slant. "I don't invite criminals into my home—or their spawn, either."

"My father didn't mean to upset anyone. You see, my parents have suffered financial setbacks lately and—"

"Shut up!" His shout echoes off the walls of the entryway. "I do not care about your setbacks. Angus MacTaggart stole from me, and I will have him prosecuted to the fullest extent of the law."

"I'll make sure he never bothers you again. Please, don't send him to prison. I will make restitution in whatever way you feel is appropriate."

Kendrick smacks both palms onto my chest and shoves so hard that I stumble backward into the door. "Take yourself away from me. I have nothing else to say. Leave before I decide to shatter your jaw with my fist."

He won't relent. I might be stubborn and desperate, but I know when I'm fighting a losing battle. The *tolla-thon* wants to punish my father. I suspect he's the sort who enjoys punishing everyone he deems to be weaker than himself. Can anyone change his mind? I drive back to my house and ring my cousin Rory, who recently finished his traineeship and became a solicitor. He's one of the cleverest and most determined people I know, so I hope he can help my family and talk Kendrick out of imprisoning my father. Rory offers to represent Da—and to speak to Rhys Kendrick.

But Rory has no better luck. From what he tells me, I think my cousin just avoided getting into a barnie with the *tolla-thon* that would've sent him to jail too. I appreciate that he tried. MacTaggarts always help each other, no matter what. The fact that sometimes our efforts fail doesn't diminish our commitment to each other.

The next day, Rhys Kendrick invites me to his house. He says he wants to offer me "an alternative solution" to the problem of my father and the item he stole. Since even a solicitor couldn't do much, I feel I have to meet with Kendrick and hear his offer. Even if Da can handle prison, Ma might not survive being separated from him again and suffering the shame of what he's done.

When I arrive at Kendrick's mansion, the man himself opens the door and ushers me inside. We go into a study where he takes the big leather chair behind the desk and I sit on a much smaller chair across from him. I see gold and silver items on shelves, decorative pieces that must've cost a ruddy fortune but that serve no useful purpose other than to make a rich scunner feel important.

Kendrick leans back in his chair, hooking one ankle over the other knee, and nails his gaze to mine. "Here's my offer. I will rescind my complaint against your father and make sure the charges are dropped—if you do a favor for me."

No, I don't like the sound of that. A favor? For a *bod ceann* like him? But I need to save my father. Maybe if I hadn't spent weeks drowning my misery in alcohol and women, I could've stopped my father from taking such drastic action to protect his family. This is my fault, and I will make it right.

"What sort of favor?" I ask.

"I want you to authenticate an artifact for me."

Oh no, that's not suspicious at all. "What sort of artifact is it?"

"Agree to do this, and I will show it to you."

For a moment, I stare at him and consider my options. I have none. "All right. I'll do it."

Kendrick smirks. "Come with me, then."

He reaches under the lip of his desk, presumably to flick a switch since a section of wall to my left slides open. I follow Kendrick into the space revealed by the hidden door. Ancient artifacts rest on shelves.

Rhys Kendrick approaches an artifact that lies atop a pedestal, sets his hand on the edge, and turns toward me. "Here it is."

I amble up to the pedestal and study the object. It's a marble statue carved in the style of similar examples I'd seen in museums and in the field years ago. "This looks like a Neolithic idol, most likely from Greece."

And it looks like a fake to me. I'm hardly an expert on the Neolithic in Greece, but during my years in the field I'd learned how to spot a forgery.

Kendrick smirks again.

But that expression crumbles when I say, "The statue is a forgery. I can't authenticate it."

The brute's eyes narrow, his nostrils flare, and he slams his fist down on the pedestal so hard that the statue wobbles and nearly tumbles off. I catch it before that happens and set the item back where it belongs.

Kendrick glowers at me. "I know the fucking thing is a forgery. But you will authenticate it if you want to free your father. Who knows what might happen to him in prison? Accidents, brawls, or worse."

It doesn't take a genius to figure out he means to guarantee those "accidents" happen if I refuse his demand. His tone makes that clear.

"Here's what you need to know," he says, "to ensure your continued cooperation. I own the original artifact that is identical to the forgery. But I need you to authenticate the fake so I can pay someone to steal it and then file an insurance claim for the full value of the genuine version—over fifty thousand pounds, according to my estimates."

"Why not just pretend the original was stolen? Why create a fake?"

"Because I want to bilk the insurance company. It's the thrill of getting away with something, don't you see?"

Kendrick's plan is nonsense, but I won't point that out. If he plans to claim the forgery was stolen, he doesn't need the fake at all. He could use a picture of the genuine artifact to commit his insurance fraud. This man is more than off his head. He's a bloody stupid ersehole of the most dangerous kind. I can't risk my family's well-being. I must do what Kendrick wants. His eyes have lit up with a perverse glee that suggests nothing will dissuade him. This man takes pleasure from cheating despite the fact he clearly doesn't need the money.

"You're in too deep to back out now, MacTaggart," he snarls.

Maybe I am. He seems like the sort who would batter me bloody if I tried to end this charade right now. Ever since I came home from America, I've made dreadful decisions. This is just one more. Might as well take my self-destruction to the final level and commit a crime myself. Like father, like son. Kendrick brings out a document that I sign. I've confirmed, in writing, that the forgery is the genuine artifact. Rhys Kendrick has won. I'm an accessory to a crime or something like that. I don't know the official terminology.

Instead of dropping the charges, though, Kendrick urges the police to move forward with them. And at the trial, he convinces the judge that a repeat offender deserves harsher punishment.

My father is sentenced to three years in prison.

All I can do is take care of my mother until Da is released. No one knows what I'd done for Kendrick, and they never will. But I'll have to live with the knowledge for the rest of my life. It's just as well that I lost Rae. She deserves a man who can take care of her and who would never debase himself the way I have—and I did it all for nothing.

From this moment forward, I will do everything possible to make up for my mistakes and become a better man.

Chapter Sixteen

Nine months after Iain vanished, on the day after Valentine's, our daughter is born. When my mom drove me to the hospital, I made her promise to go home and retrieve the scarf Iain had given me. I had planned never to look at the thing again, but when I realized I was about to give birth, I suddenly needed to have that scarf with me. Mom didn't complain. She rushed home to get it.

Now I lie in a hospital bed with my daughter in my arms and Iain's scarf wrapped around her tiny body. I just hold her for a while—a long while, actually—while tears stream down my cheeks and I gaze at her sweet face. These tears represent the joy of meeting my child at last and the grief of realizing her father will never know her.

"Look," I tell my mom. "She has pale blue eyes like Iain."

"A lot of babies are born with blue eyes, but the color might change later."

"No, her eyes will stay like this." Maybe I want that because it means a sliver of Iain will always be with me. Yeah, it's pathetic. But I can't help that I still love him. "I already know what I want to call her."

"I've seen you poring over books of baby names. You didn't know I saw, but I did." My mother moves over to sit on the bed's edge right beside me. She gazes down at my daughter and smiles. "Whatever name you've chosen will be the right one. And I know this girl will be as good and strong as her mother."

And she will be like Iain too. I believe that, though I can't explain why. So I kiss my daughter's forehead and say, "Her name is Malina."

"That's beautiful, Rae."

I won't confess that I chose that name because it's the feminine form of Malcolm, Iain's middle name. Choosing the feminine version of his first name seemed too obvious. Once I found the name Malina, I knew that's what I would call my child if I had a daughter. I hadn't wanted to know the baby's sex beforehand, but I hoped for a little girl.

My parents' divorce had been finalized last year, four months after Iain vanished, and Mom used the settlement to buy us a house in Texas—a new home for me, Mom, and Malina, in a place far from where all those bad things happened. We now live in the Hill Country, where wildflowers bloom in the rolling green fields every spring, heralding a new beginning. We need that. Mom is divorced, and I lost the love of my life, so starting over here feels like the best thing that's ever happened to us.

Though Mom says she doesn't care how long I take to decide what I want to do with my life, I realize I need to come up with a plan soon. I have a child to take care of, after all. Our new house came with plenty of acreage, so I could do something with that. But it takes me a few weeks to settle on a plan. Then I sit down with Mom to explain it all.

"I want to raise sheep," I tell her. "For the wool. I did a lot of research, and there's a big market for wool these days. Lots of shops sell genuine wool yarn for people who want to ditch the synthetics and go natural."

"You really have researched this, haven't you?"

"Want me to recite all the statistics I've learned about the wool industry in the US?"

Mom laughs. "No, sweetie, I believe you. One thing I know about my daughter is that she's smart enough to do anything she sets her mind to."

"Starting an at-home business will also give me the chance to spend as much as time as I can with Malina."

"You're a wonderful mother, Rae." Mom clasps my hand. "I'll help you however I can. Anything you need, just ask. And it goes without saying that I'm your on-call, in-house babysitter."

"Thanks, Mom."

Will my plan work? I'm about to learn the answer. My mother provides the working capital to get started, but she sank most of her divorce settlement into buying this property. I don't want to empty her savings account, but she insists on giving me whatever I need. I can't secure a loan on my own, so to get the rest of the capital, I create an LLC with Mom as my partner. With her on board, our local bank agrees to loan us what we need. I can't believe I'm doing this. But like Mom often reminds me, Everhart women never give up. We strap on our mud boots and our overalls and climb into the muck.

Maybe I lost the only man I ever loved, but I've found my true love at last. She's six months old and the sweetest little girl in the world. Every time I feel like I can't make the business work, I look at my daughter—and then I know I can and I will succeed.

Though Mom offered to babysit, right now I prefer to keep Malina with me as much as possible. I get a baby carrier thingy that straps onto my chest like a reverse backpack. That way, I can survey the property with my daughter and my mom too. We figure out where the property line is and devise a plan for the sheep pasture and the paddocks we'll need too. We hire some guys to put up the fencing and to build an addition to the existing barn.

Months roll by, and finally, it's time for the sheep to arrive.

Sometimes I think about Iain and wonder how he would feel about my new life. But it's only a fleeting thought. I'm too busy to worry about the past.

On the day the sheep arrive, Malina has just turned ten months old. She walks like a pro now, and she gets so excited about the sheep. Mom keeps hold of Malina while I oversee the unloading of the sheep. They arrived in a huge trailer pulled by a massive pickup truck, much bigger than the one I've got. But I won't need to transport the sheep, so I don't need a heavy-duty vehicle.

After the big day, it's back to the grindstone.

Two months later, we celebrate Malina's first birthday. Later, on the day that marks exactly two years since Iain disappeared from my life, I allow myself to wallow a little bit.

Mom has taken Malina outside to visit the sheep, which the kiddo always loves to do. While they have fun, I go inside to dig out the scarf Iain had given me on Valentine's Day back in Nackington. I also find the photo strip from that booth in the mall. Wrapping the scarf around me, I gaze at the pictures. Tears dribble down my cheeks, but I'm not in any danger of sobbing. These are goodbye tears. The time has come to lay the memories to rest and enjoy the rest of my life with only the occasional thoughts of Iain MacTaggart. I feel freer afterward, and I stuff the scarf into the back of a drawer. But I put the photo strip into a little photo album I've been making that documents important moments in Malina's life. Then I shove that into the drawer too.

Why? Because that album isn't for me and Mom and Malina. It's for Iain. Not that I think he'll ever see it, but I've given up on fighting the impulse to save something for him, just in case. I take a lot of pictures of our daughter. Some go into the family album, while a select few make it into the one for Iain. Will I ever use this album? It's doubtful. Moving on doesn't mean I can't save a few memories for the man who gave me the most incredible gift I've ever received—our daughter, who will always remind me of her father.

As the years pass, I occasionally date, though nothing much comes of it. I never bring men to the house, and my daughter will never meet or even know about them. Even my mom doesn't know the details. Of course, for safety's sake, I tell her when and where I'm going when I have a date. If I sleep with a guy, though, I keep that to myself. After a while, I give up on romance. It just doesn't interest me anymore.

Seven years after we moved to Texas, Mom meets a wonderful man. Soon, they're married—and I have a stepfather, a stepbrother, and a stepsister. Malina adores them all, and so do I. At least one of the Everhart women managed to find Prince Charming and get that happily ever after. Mom now lives in California, but we see each other several times a year, either with me and Malina flying to California, or Mom and her new family coming here. Greg, my stepfather, is such a good man that I never even think about my real dad anymore.

Yeah, life is looking pretty damn wonderful these days.

When Malina turns ten, I let Mom talk me into "getting out there" again. A few more bad dates later, I'm ready to throw in the towel. Then I meet a man who seems like a nice guy and says all the right things—when we're in bed. I hired him as my ranch hand, but we sneak away to motels to have sex. My time with Grayson Parker is the closest I've come to having a relationship since that Scottish man whose name I've completely forgotten. Okay, even I know that's not true. I only think of Iain now because Grayson just dumped me. The second I suggested he could come to my house to meet my daughter, he scrammed at sixty miles an hour. The jerk actually told me he didn't want to play daddy to some other guy's castoff.

Nobody refers to my daughter that way.

I hear the loser now drives a taxi. The nearest town isn't large, which means he probably doesn't get much work. Is it wrong to feel a tiny flush of triumph about that? The ass did call my daughter a "castoff." Oh yeah, I'm better off without that moron in my life. I still see him occasionally, but we ignore each other as much as possible. My latest mistake will be my last. No more men. Who needs them? In the romantic sense, I mean. I don't hate all members of the opposite sex.

The new ranch hand I hire does not want to date me. Ben has a girlfriend. He's also incredibly kind and sweet, not to mention a hard worker. We've become good friends. Mom loves Ben, and so does Malina.

Can't believe my little girl will turn twelve next year.

Greg and Mom invite me and Malina to go to Bermuda with their gang. Malina is so excited she actually jumps up and down while clapping her hands and grinning. How can I say no? We get passports and pack our bags, ready to go in two days.

But Ben breaks his arm.

That means Malina and I have to skip the big trip. I know she's disappointed, but being an Everhart girl, she doesn't let it keep her down. Besides, I buy her an iPod to make up for it. After that, she doesn't care about Bermuda anymore.

On the day after Valentine's, Malina turns twelve. Since our California family couldn't make it here to celebrate with us, I make sure my baby gets all the presents she wanted and her favorite cake—chocolate with vanilla frosting and vanilla ice cream. She inherited that preference from me. But after the party is over and the presents are all unwrapped, after Malina has gone to bed too, I allow myself to wallow just a teeny bit.

That means I excavate from the depths of my dresser two items, the photo album and the scarf made from the MacTaggart clan tartan. I add a new photo to the album, one that shows Malina blowing out the twelve candles on her birthday cake. I pull out the photo strip that had been tucked inside the album and gaze into the pale blue eyes of the man who changed my life in ways he will never know about, though I've made peace with that fact.

I will always love Iain. I've made peace with that too.

Done reminiscing, I hide those items once again. Then I head into the living room for the last itty-bitty bit of wallowing. I approach the shelves that hold numerous books about topics that hold a special meaning for me, though no one except my mom understands why. They're books about Scotland. History. Architecture. Folk beliefs. Whatever I could find, I bought it. I even own a primer on the Gaelic language, though I haven't worked my way through the whole thing yet. Most of the words Iain had used are not in that book. I couldn't remember those terms he'd used on the day we met—something about his magic staff, but in Gaelic—so I had no way to look those up. Kinda doubt they're in the book, anyway.

Oh well. The thing he used to call me that I loved the best had nothing to do with Gaelic. Now I close my eyes and let my mind travel back to those days, and I hear Iain's voice, smoky and irresistible, as he calls me "sunshine." Though I will never forget him, I've made a new life for myself.

But now that life is threatened. The wool market has been on a downward turn lately, which cuts into my profits. I could let Ben go, but I don't want to do that. I know the economy goes through ups and downs, but the slump in the wool market shows no sign of easing up. What will I do? I don't know. My income has decreased over the past three years. I've started selling some of my lambs, but only to people who want them as pets, since I can't stomach the idea of selling them for food. I eat meat, so I know I'm a hypocrite. But I see their cute little sheep faces every day. That's why I can't send them to the slaughterhouse. The money I get from selling them as pets hasn't made much of a dent in my financial problems.

I need to plan for Malina's future too, to save in case she wants to go to college. Right now, she thinks she wants to become a sheep rancher like me. But she's twelve. She'll change her mind a hundred times before she graduates from high school. I want her to have options.

Done browsing those books about Scotland, I go to bed and try not to worry about money. After an hour of tossing and turning, I realize only one thing will help me sleep. So I sink into the memories of Iain and our time at Nackington, of his smile and those blue eyes, the ones that mirror our daughter's. I remember his kisses too, the sexy way he smiled when he fed me ice cream with his mouth. But mostly, I fantasize about Iain holding me and calling me "sunshine" as well as that Scottish word he never explained—*gràidh*.

Soon, I fall asleep.

But in the morning, I realize I need to give up that crutch. I will give it up. Iain is my past.

No, I will never fantasize about him again.

Chapter Seventeen

Iain

What have I done with my life? Well, I've made a fair amount of money, enough to support my parents and ensure Da never burgles anyone ever again. Finding artifacts that had been lost to history earns me a reward every time. Rhys Kendrick does not harass me anymore. He got what he wanted, so he ought to be happy. The bastard has celebrated his victory by buying up half the village of Loch Fairbairn. Everyone knows the *bod ceann* takes advantage of store owners who have fallen on hard times, offering to buy them out with a significant settlement. I don't blame them for giving in. But whatever Rhys Kendrick means to do with those buildings, I doubt it involves improving the village.

My father spends eighteen months in prison. Well, at least he's home now. Ma took his absence better than I'd expected. Better than I did, for sure.

I wish I could say I've become a better man, but that would be a lie. I've shagged more women than I care to count, though most of those encounters were brief and happened in the early years after I came home from America. Still, I've made even worse mistakes.

First, I marry a woman I don't love and expect to feel satisfied with the situation. Julia is a sweet lass, but I have no right to use her to fill up the gaping hole in my heart. It doesn't work, anyway. After seven months of marriage, she can't take it anymore—and I don't blame her. My marriage is over.

My second mistake might be even worse.

One day, I bump into a bonnie woman in a café in Inverness. She'd been visiting the local shops to find items she could use to re-decorate her home. I went there to visit the Highland Archive Centre in hopes of uncovering information about a potential new discov-ery in the Loch Fairbairn area. The woman I meet has a familiar name—Delyth Kendrick. We share a table and get to know each other a wee bit, but that's not the problem.

Delyth seems like a lonely woman, and living with a man like Rhys can't be good for her. She won't leave him, but that's all I know. Maybe I feel sorry for her, or maybe I've reverted to my old ways, because I accept Delyth's offer to become her secret lover. Her hus-band often takes business trips, so Delyth and I meet at the Kendrick mansion whenever Rhys is away. I suspect he shags other women during his absences. Is that an excuse for my behavior? No. But I honestly like Delyth, though I know I will never develop deeper feel-ings for her. I've told her about my lost love, leaving out Rae's name and the details of our relationship, to make sure Delyth understands my limitations.

I can never love anyone else, not after Rae.

During the fifth year of our affair, I begin to pull away from De-lyth. We don't see each other as often, and I don't feel any real satisfac-tion from our encounters, except for the sexual kind. Even that isn't as good anymore.

But one day, my life changes. My cousins have asked me to take in Gavin Douglas, the boyfriend of our cousin Jamie, and let him live in my house while he sorts out the mess he made with the love of his life. I know exactly why my cousins chose me for this task. Gavin and I have taken similar paths down the wrong road, for similar reasons. I let go of Rae out of shame, because of our age difference and my father's larcenous escapades, while Gavin threw Jamie over out of shame related to his disastrous marriage to a nar-cissistic woman. He doesn't take more than a decade to realize he made a mistake, though. Gavin recognized that five minutes after he broke Jamie's heart.

So aye, I let him stay with me. We have serious discussions about his relationship with Jamie, talks that do more than help my new mate. They also make me realize that I should never have given up on Rae so easily. The years have taught me many lessons, but I didn't know until recently that the Bremner-Ashton mafia couldn't have gotten me deported. I abandoned Rae for no reason.

Jamie and Gavin reconcile, but my mate has a few choice words of wisdom for me. "It's never too late to rectify the mistakes you made. I strung Jamie along for eighteen months while I lived in America and she stayed here in Scotland. Having a relationship across an ocean could never work. Jamie didn't want to trust me again, but I never gave up—not even after I dumped her."

"Aye, but I did give up on the lass I loved. The situations aren't the same."

"Not on every point. But we're both stubborn morons. Don't give up on your girl until you're one hundred percent sure there's no chance."

I exhale a long sigh. "It's been almost thirteen years. Ahmno likely to find her now."

"Have you tried? I mean, like, really tried?" He lays a hand on my shoulder. "Listen, I know it's a damn scary thing to do, trying to reconnect after all these years. But if there's one lesson you can learn from me, it's that you have to let go of the fear and shame. Just do it, Iain. If I could let Jamie's brothers hound me for two months to prove I was serious about their sister, you can bite that bullet and look for Rae."

"You're right, I know." I rub my jaw. "Let me think on it."

"Okay. But don't think too much."

With Gavin's experience as a guide, I should begin my quest. But I waste two months worrying about it before I finally I realize what I need to do. Finding Rae had felt like a goal I could never achieve, until I remembered what I have on my side. The MacTaggart clan, that's what. Not only my blood relatives, but the Americans they've married as well. The lasses who tied the knot with my cousins Lachlan, Aidan, and Rory started an official organization to meddle in other people's lives. They call it the American Wives Club. Those lasses took matters into their own hands with Jamie and Gavin, rallying anyone and everyone in the MacTaggart family to get it done.

Can they help me find Rae? I decide to ask Rory about that.

"You don't need the American Wives Club," he says when I ring him. "Whatever it is you think you need, discuss it with me first. I have connections at the Home Office and in America too."

He invites me to his office to discuss the matter. On the following day, February fifteenth, I walk into his office. The room is a mess, which would never have happened before Rory married Emery. The bonnie American lass has cured my cousin of his uptight tendencies.

Rory invites me to sit down and takes a seat in the big chair behind the desk, then the discussion begins. When I admit that I've been slightly jealous of Rory and the other men in the clan who have found their soul mates, he gives me a strange look.

"Jealous of what?" he asks. "You have more than enough money, you do what you want when you want, and you can have any woman you want."

"Aye, any woman I want. Except the only one who matters."

The more we talk, the more I realize Rory is trying to wheedle the truth out of me delicately, the way I imagine a solicitor often needs to do.

"We all know something happened to you in America, but you've never wanted to talk about it," he finally says. "Is this about a woman? The MacTaggart grapevine has embellished the story over the years, but it all began with what Kevin Lister claimed he heard you say at a pub one night."

"Yes," I say, trying to sound calm despite the acid boiling in my gut. "I lost a woman. No, that's not quite right. I gave her up without a fight, and I've regretted it ever since."

Rory raises a Valentine's card and turns it so I can see the words his wife scrawled inside it. *Love is a journey from pain to redemption. Never forget how far we've come.*

My throat grows tight and thick, but I manage an even tone. "What am I meant to take away from your wife's effusive love for you? It's charming but—"

"Never give up. That's the lesson." Rory sets down the card. "Tell me more about your woman."

Rory goes on trying to convince me that I need to try to find Rae, and that I deserve a second chance. But why would a vital young woman want me? I'm fifty years old. She must be thirty-five now. For all I know, she already has a husband and children. But Rory doesn't give up. He keeps pushing me to admit what we both know I want—to see Rae again.

When he asks for the name of the woman, I hesitate for only a moment before I take a deep breath and tell him. "Rae Everhart."

Then he instructs me to write down everything I can remember about her. While I do that, a sort of excitement I've never experienced in my entire life electrifies me because, for the first time in thirteen years, I have a chance to see Rae and at least apologize to her. I leave Rory's office with his assurances he will contact whoever he must in order to track down the lass.

After four months, I've ignored Rory's advice and given up. Rory's investigator had called yesterday to tell me he's had no luck tracking down Rae. Though I'd stopped sleeping with Delyth after my cousin convinced me he could find my lost love, now I crawl back to my former lover and try to lose myself inside her body, but it doesn't work. I still think about Rae.

Eight days later, I receive the news I've dreamed of hearing. The investigator Rory hired has found Rae at last.

A weight has lifted off me, and I feel almost lightheaded from the knowledge that I can see her again, speak to her again, find out if she thought of me every day for the past thirteen years just the way I'd thought of her. Rory lends me his private jet so I can get to America faster. My journey doesn't end there, though. Since the car hire agency at the airport had no vehicles available, I jump into a taxi and ask to be taken to the address Rory had found for Rae, though he couldn't swear she still lives there or that it's the right Rae Everhart. Her driver's license gave this as her address, but the property is owned by Cheryl Raines. The taxi driver takes me from Austin to Llano, the farthest he can go. Then I find a second taxi for the next part of my journey, which ends at a small town called Ricksville. For the third and final leg of my quest, I ride in a rickety taxi with a surly driver. But he boots me out of the car at the end of Rae's driveway.

"Hope you're in better shape than you look," he says in a snide tone. "You've got a half-mile walk to get to the house, and ambulances don't come out this far."

I throw my large bag over my shoulder, pay the driver, and start down the half-mile-long gravel drive. My felt fedora shields my eyes, but it makes my head sweat too. Maybe I'm no young laddie, but I can handle the walk. For the chance to see Rae again, I will endure any hardship.

Finally, I reach a metal gate that has a latch holding it shut. After crossing through the gate and shutting it behind me, I notice a figure up ahead. A woman. My pulse accelerates, and I suddenly have trouble pulling in a full breath. It's not exhaustion, though. I swear that's Rae waiting for me, though I cannae even see her face yet. I keep my head down as I traipse across the last stretch of the drive. Though I notice a house and a barn, nothing else catches my attention once I lay eyes on Rae.

"Hey!" she shouts. "Stop! This is private property."

I pause to remove my hat so I can swipe a hand over my forehead. Sweat has dribbled down my temples. I continue striding toward Rae until I stand an arm's length from the lass, then I drop my bag on the ground and smile. "Rae Everhart. It's been a long time, but I found you."

The lass just stares at me slack-jawed.

Well, I have arrived with no warning after thirteen years away from her.

She swallows hard enough that I can see the movement. "Iain?"

"I've waited thirteen years for this. Can't wait a second longer."

I close the distance between us, sling an arm around her waist, and drag her into my body.

"Whuh—"

I silence whatever she'd been about to say with my lips. She has stronger muscles than before, and I love the feel of them against me. Her lips are soft and warm, and the slightest flavor of her teases me, though I don't even try to deepen the kiss. Not yet. I've only just found her again, and we'll need time to get reacquainted. Even after I peel my lips away from hers, she keeps her eyes closed. Aye, Rae did that often on the day when I'd finally kissed her after ten months of waiting. I couldn't stop then, and I donnae want to stop now. But we need to talk.

Still holding her close, I murmur, "You have no idea how happy I am to see you, Rae. You're even more beautiful than the last time I saw you."

The lass shoves me away. "What on earth do you think you're doing? You can't waltz up my driveway, invite yourself through the gate, and then kiss me."

"But I did, and you let me." I grab my hat off the ground, though I don't remember dropping it. Kissing Rae distracted me. I dust my hat off. "I came a long way to see you."

"And that gives you the right to barge into my life?"

She tugs her shirt down and squares her shoulders, giving me the stubborn look I remember well. "Iain, go home. Turn around and walk back the way you came."

"Afraid I can't." I slap the fedora back onto my head. "I'm not leaving until you've heard me out."

She stares at me for a long moment. Then she spins around and stalks over to the house and up the steps onto the porch. She shuts the front door behind her.

Does she honestly think that will stop me? I jog over there and spring over the steps to land on the porch floor. Then I approach the door and shout, "I'll wait out here until you change your mind."

I receive no response.

"Rae," I shout at the door. "I'm asking for a few minutes, that's all."

The door swings open, and Rae steps aside, waving an arm. "Get in here and say whatever it is you think you need to say. I'll listen, but you will leave once you're done. No arguments. When I say go, you go."

I tip my hat to her. "Whatever you say."

Hat in hand, I follow her into the house and cannae resist admiring her bonnie erse along the way. When she closes the door, I drop my bag on the floor with a rather loud thunk. Maybe I had over-packed slightly. The only thing of any real value inside that bag is the diamond engagement ring I'd bought for her thirteen years ago.

Rae faces me, her brows raised and her arms crossed.

Bod an Donais, I want to ravish her with a kiss hotter than the Texas sun. I'll do that in a few minutes. First, I need to tell her the truth. "What I have to say is simple. I never should've let you go without a fight, and I won't make that mistake again. I've come to win you back, Rae."

No matter what I must do, no matter how long this takes, I will win back the heart of the only woman I've ever loved. The journey that brought me here began thirteen years ago, but it ends today. I will fight for our second chance the way I should've fought for Rae more than a decade ago. Whatever it takes, however long I need to struggle to convince Rae she can trust me, I will succeed.

Aye, we will have our fairy-tale ending.

**Find out how Iain helped Gavin win back Jamie
in *Gift-Wrapped in a Kilt* (Hot Scots, Book Four),
then experience Iain and Rae's story
in *Notorious in a Kilt* (Hot Scots, Book Five).**

Anna Durand is a bestselling, multi-award-winning author of contemporary and paranormal romance. Her books have earned bestseller status on every major retailer and wonderful reviews from readers around the world. But that's the boring spiel. Here are the really cool things you want to know about Anna!

Born on Lackland Air Force Base in Texas, Anna grew up moving here, there, and everywhere thanks to her dad's job as an instructor pilot. She's lived in Texas (twice), Mississippi, California (twice), Michigan (twice), and Alaska—and now Ohio.

As for her writing, Anna has always made up stories in her head, but she didn't write them down until her teen years. Those first awful books went into the trash can a few years later, though she learned a lot from those stories. Eventually, she would pen her first romance novel, the paranormal romance *Willpower*, and she's never looked back since.

Want even more details about Anna? Get access to her extended bio when you subscribe to her newsletter and download the free bonus ebook, *Hot Scots Confidential.* You'll also get hot deleted scenes, character interviews, fun facts, and more! Plus you'll receive audio bonus content narrated by Shane East, Vanessa Edwin, and Ava Lucas.

Visit AnnaDurand.com to sign up.